IN THE JUNGLES OF THE NIGHT

Also by Stephen Alter

NON-FICTION

*Becoming a Mountain: Himalayan Journeys in Search of the
Sacred and the Sublime*

All the Way to Heaven: An American Boyhood in the Himalayas

Amritsar to Lahore: Crossing the Border between India and Pakistan

Sacred Waters: A Pilgrimage to the Many Sources of the Ganga

Elephas Maximus: A Portrait of the Indian Elephant

*Going For Take: The Making of Omkara and
Other Encounters in Bollywood*

FICTION

Neglected Lives

Silk and Steel

The Godchild

Renuka

Aripan and Other Stories

Aranyani

The Phantom Isles

Ghost Letters

The Rataban Betrayal

The Secret Sanctuary

IN THE JUNGLES OF THE NIGHT

A NOVEL ABOUT JIM CORBETT

STEPHEN ALTER

ALEPH

ALEPH

ALEPH BOOK COMPANY
An independent publishing firm
promoted by *Rupa Publications India*

First published in India in 2016
by Aleph Book Company
7/16 Ansari Road, Daryaganj
New Delhi 110 002

ISBN: 978-93-83064-67-0

1 3 5 7 9 10 8 6 4 2

For sale in the Indian subcontinent only.

Printed by Parksons Graphics Pvt. Ltd, Mumbai

In memory of
Kavi Singh

Tyger, tyger, burning bright
In the forests of the night;
What immortal hand or eye,
Dare frame thy fearful symmetry?

WILLIAM BLAKE

Human beings are not the natural prey of
tigers, and it is only when tigers have been
incapacitated through wounds or old age
that, in order to live, they are compelled
to take to a diet of human flesh.

JIM CORBETT, *Man-eaters of Kumaon*

CONTENTS

A NOTE ON JIM CORBETT

Jim Corbett was a legendary hunter and naturalist best known for killing a number of man-eating tigers and leopards in the foothills of Kumaon, in northern India. He was born in the hill station of Nainital in 1875 and lived there until 1947, when he left India at the time of independence and settled in Nyeri, Kenya, where he died in 1955. Corbett never married and lived most of his life in the company of his sister, Maggie, who was a year older than him. He wrote a series of bestselling books, which includes *Man-eaters of Kumaon* and *Jungle Lore*. During his lifetime, Jim Corbett was hailed as a modern-day 'dragon slayer', and he was honoured by villagers and viceroys alike. His knowledge of natural history and jungle craft allowed him to take up wildlife photography in his later years, when he had all but set aside his rifles. Corbett was one of the first persons to take cine-films of tigers in the wild. A patriotic Englishman, he volunteered in both World Wars and taught courses in survival training to Allied officers on the Burma front, for which he was given the honorary rank of colonel. Today, one of India's largest national parks and tiger reserves near Corbett's winter home in Kaladhungi bears his name. He has been honoured with postage stamps as well as statues, and a subspecies of tiger in Southeast Asia is named *Panthera tigris corbetti*. While this book draws upon many of Corbett's stories and historical facts surrounding his life, it is a work of fiction and does not aspire to any pretence of biographical surety.

I

THE FERN COLLECTOR
1888

ONE

Here in the clouds, Jim could feel an unsettling sense of communion. Monsoon mist spilled through the branches of deodar and cypress trees. No mountains were visible, only a cowl of murky white, obscuring the ridgelines, the lake and the tops of the taller trees. Jim's hair was wet from the veil of moisture. The rain had stopped but his rough cotton shirt felt damp and droplets of water clung to the blonde hairs on his arms.

He had come to the graveyard alone. There were leeches this time of year and patches of stinging nettle growing between the headstones. His father—Christopher William Corbett—was buried in the cemetery. He had died seven years ago on 21 April 1881, when Jim was only six. Out of habit more than grief, he had stopped at his father's grave and run his fingers lightly over the inscription, as if he were reading Braille.

Many of the headstones in the cemetery dated from 1880, when the great Nainital landslip claimed 151 lives—108 Indians along with 43 British subjects. Most of the Christian victims were dug out of the debris from the mudslide and reburied in the cemetery next to St John in the Wilderness Church, on the Mallital side of town. This catastrophe was one of Jim's earliest memories and he could remember listening to the cannonade of rain on their sheet metal roof, non-stop for two days, and then hearing anxious voices calling out in the storm. The next day he was led by his sister Maggie to a point beyond the garden fence, where they could see a massive scar on the hillside where the mountain had collapsed, consuming homes and hutments as well as part of the Naina Devi temple at the western end of the lake.

Neat rows of gravestones were laid out on terraces below the church. The claustrophobic whiteness of the mist was combed by bristling needles of deodars. Jim tried to imagine what it would be like to die in a landslip, buried alive and suffocated by mud. A peacock orchid grew near his father's headstone. Its purple petals stood out amidst the plush green moss like a gaudy exclamation mark.

The swirling mist made Jim think of ghosts, not an individual phantom but a collective spirit emerging from dozens of separate graves and mingling together in a haunting embrace. While each headstone bore the last remnants of identity—names, dates of birth and death, as well as a scripture verse—the mist carried no such markers. At this early hour, soon after daybreak on a Saturday morning, nobody else was around. Jim felt as if he might be the last person on earth, alone within a condensed fog of tears. He almost wanted to shout, or sing, or whistle to chase off the loneliness.

He had come to the graveyard for a purpose that had nothing to do with crumbling memorials or uneasy mysteries of the afterlife. Jim was gathering ferns for his botany collection, uprooting specimens and carrying these in a small jute bag. Later, he would press the ferns, their delicate filigree dried and preserved. So far, he had found six different species—two kinds of polypods, a male fern, maidenhair, common lip, and a Bible fern that looked like a triangle of green lace. More than any of these, he was searching for a mouse-ear fern, which was rare. Jim had seen one in a collection at school, the brittle specimen stuck to the yellowing pages of an album, its scientific name written in faded ink—*Gymnopteris vestita*. As he picked his way between the graves, Jim scanned the terraces for the distinctive shape of those fronds, like miniature green ears listening to his approach.

A few bird calls could be heard, the mournful wailing of a great Himalayan barbet and the tremulous shriek of a whistling thrush. The birds remained unseen and the sounds seemed far away in the mist. He thought of the cries of buried souls beneath the slurry of rubble and collapsed homes. For two days after the landslide, voices could be heard calling out for help as men dug desperately with pickaxes and shovels. Few of the victims were rescued alive.

Beyond his father's grave, he climbed a set of shallow slate steps to the next level, passing a tilted cross and stooping to avoid the lower branches of an oak. As he raised his head and glanced around, he could see the wall of the cemetery built along the contour of the hill. Layers of mist sloughed off in the breeze. Jim could just make out the Gothic bell tower of the church where he had been baptized fourteen years ago. Twenty feet above him, on a higher terrace, he spotted something strange—a pile of dirt.

Hesitating, Jim stepped around another gravestone, then scrambled up a section of the hill where a retaining wall had collapsed. He caught sight of an unusual fern growing out of the fallen stones but didn't stop. A new grave seemed to have been dug...but here, in a forgotten corner of the cemetery? Most of the recent graves were down below, including Miss Coles': she had taught him maths last year and died of typhoid fever this spring. Jim had attended her funeral, along with everyone else at Petersfield School. In this section the graves were not as recent, going back at least ten years, before the great landslip. There were soldiers and merchants, memsahibs and infants, civil servants and missionaries who had lived and died in Nainital from the time it was first settled by the British in 1841.

Climbing cautiously, Jim could clearly see the mound of freshly turned earth. Pulling himself up with the help of a cypress branch, an uncomfortable sensation passed over the back of his neck and shoulders as if someone had brushed his skin with a dry fern. He glanced around but nobody was in sight. By now, the curtains of mist had drawn closer, so that he could see only a few yards ahead.

The hole in the ground looked as if it had been dug in a hurry. The dirt was a dull, reddish colour from iron in the soil. Several tree roots had been exposed and hacked. Peering into the grave, Jim winced and took a step back. Inside were the rotted remains of a coffin, broken boards pulled apart, nails twisted. The pit was six feet deep and the box had been tipped to one side. It was empty. Someone had removed the corpse or skeleton—whatever was left of the person buried there. Jim leaned forward again and searched the tomb with his eyes but he could see no trace of human remains.

Whoever had taken the body must have come here last night or early
in the morning, long before dawn. A puddle of rain had collected at
the bottom of the grave. The mud was marked by smeared footprints,
some with shoes and some without. The naked impressions of bare
toes and heels looked almost obscene.

He felt an impulse to run away, the nerves in his arms and legs
twitching, his breath sucked in, teeth clenched. Jim nearly dropped
the bag full of ferns. Yet something held him here, as if he were
trapped by the mist, an infinite white glove that closed in around
him and made it impossible to move. Beyond the pile of dirt, he
caught sight of the headstone, which had been dragged aside. A
rectangular slab of granite, it was lying at an angle, half-buried by
mud excavated from the grave. Though the stone was blemished
with leprous patches of lichens, Jim could easily read the inscription
after brushing away the dirt.

In Loving Memory of
Cynthia Lily Bertram
Dearest Daughter—Beloved Sister
Born: 2 May, 1859 Died: 7 April, 1878

The Lord is my light and my salvation; whom shall I fear?
Psalms 27:1

'*She was killed by a leopard,*' *Reverend Olten explained, his voice hoarse* with phlegm. Taking out a wrinkled handkerchief, he blew his nose and examined the results before folding it away in the frayed pocket of his dressing gown.

'Was it a man-eater?' Jim asked.

The old man eyed him with impatience.

'That's enough, James,' his mother said.

Mary Jane Corbett had brought her son to the vicarage as soon as Jim told her what he had discovered in the cemetery. She had left her daughters to make breakfast for the other children and set off on foot. Reverend Olten was the pastor at St John in the Wilderness Church. He and his wife lived down the hill from the sanctuary. The vicarage was a dark, dank bungalow, smelling of mildew, spoiled mangoes and wet laundry. One of the oldest residents of Nainital, William Olten was long past the age when most people retired and went back home to England. A cold had settled in his chest and when he coughed it sounded like cardboard being torn to shreds. They waited until he finished and blew his nose again. Very little light came in through the windows but Jim could see how red the pastor's eyes looked, bloodshot and feverish.

'A tragedy,' Reverend Olten began, whispering through chapped lips. 'Cindy Bertram disappeared one evening as she was walking on the south side of the lake, near Smuggler's Rock. One or two people had met her a few minutes before and then she was gone. Her father was down on the plains—he worked in the railways—but her mother had brought the children up for the season and put the boys in Philander Smith's School and the girls at All Saints. When

Cindy didn't return home that evening, Colleen Bertram went over to a neighbour's house and they raised an alarm. At first we thought the poor girl might have fallen down the khud or slipped into the lake and drowned, but there was no sign of her. All night we sent out search parties. I can still hear the voices calling her name and the lanterns waving in the dark. It was early April and bitterly cold…' Once again, the pastor began to cough and turned his face aside. Jim could see the white bristle on his unshaven jowls and the wrinkled skin on his neck.

They were waiting for Inspector Edwin Pearson, the station house officer, to arrive. Reverend Olten was in no condition to visit the graveyard himself and he had sent a note to the police station. The pastor's wife entered from the kitchen. Nellie Olten was a tall, stern woman with steel-grey curls. She wore a stained white apron over a grey dress. As her husband recovered from his coughing fit, she picked up the story.

'We didn't find her that night or the next day. It was only forty-eight hours later, that one of the forest guards discovered Cindy's body. She was down in a ravine, two miles beyond Sukha Tal, along the Kaladhungi Road. Crows and magpies were feeding on the corpse, which is how the guard found her. The body had been badly mauled and her dress was torn. They covered her with a tablecloth from Sorrel Lodge before bringing her up to the Bertrams' house. At first, they were going to take her to the hospital but it was decided there was no need for a post-mortem. She was buried before her father arrived, for the corpse was already decomposing. Her mother, Colleen, was silent the whole time and didn't shed a tear, staring at the carpet as if in a trance. Cindy had a twin brother too. Isaac… It was heartbreaking to see a family face such horror…' Mrs Olten paused. 'Of course, there were those who said it wasn't a leopard…'

'Hush, Nellie,' Reverend Olten's voice croaked from the depths of his overstuffed chair but his wife ignored him. He himself would be dead from pneumonia in another month.

'I don't mean to gossip, but there were some who believed she was murdered and it was made to look like a leopard's kill.' Nellie

Olten rubbed the raw, red knuckles on her hands. Jim could see that her fingers were thick as a man's.

'Why would she have been murdered?' he asked, standing beside his mother's chair, with his cap in one hand.

'It was just talk,' Mary Jane said.

'Who knows?' said Mrs Olten, shrugging her stooped shoulders.

'But then why would someone dig up her grave after all these years?' Jim asked.

The adults stared at him with expressions of disapproval. His mother's eyes bore a look of anxious warning, while Reverend Olten's conveyed bloodshot suspicion. The pastor's wife squinted at Jim, as if it were his fault.

'We'll have to wait and find out,' Mary Jane Corbett said. 'It's a terrible thing, whatever the reason.'

Earlier, after running home from the cemetery, Jim's fears had subsided, replaced by curiosity and excitement. But now, sitting in the Oltens' drawing room with the musty furniture and dingy drapes half-covering the windows, he began to feel uncomfortable again. A large spider carrying a white egg sac crawled up the wall, where damp stains showed under the ceiling. Of course, he'd already heard about Cindy Bertram being killed by a leopard. It was an old story everyone in Nainital knew. Mothers often used it to urge their children indoors before dark. Jim felt a current of fear run down his arms and legs as he recalled the empty grave, the boards of the coffin torn apart, as if some creature, maybe even a leopard, had ripped it open. At the same time, he kept seeing in his mind the human footprints in the mud.

'Someone should inform the family,' Mrs Olten said. 'Would anyone know where they are?'

'Bertrams were mixed blood,' said the pastor, with a judgemental cough. 'Maybe the Tunneys will know.'

'I think I've got Colleen's address,' Mary Jane said. 'She lives in Aligarh. Her husband died and she remarried...someone in the canal service, I believe.'

Just then there was a loud knock and the sound of men's voices.

Mrs Olten went across to open the front door. Inspector Pearson entered, leaving an umbrella on the veranda. His khaki uniform was speckled with rain. Once again, Jim had to explain what he'd seen and answer the same volley of questions. *What was he doing at the graveyard? Fern collecting? Alone? When did he discover the grave? Was anyone else around? Was the coffin disturbed? No sign of the body?* He tried to recount everything as accurately as he could.

'I'll have to take your statement and file a report,' Pearson said, 'but first we'll go and have a look ourselves.' Then he turned back towards Jim. 'All right, boy, you won't mind coming with us, will you?'

Jim nodded before glancing at his mother.

'I'll come too,' she said.

As they stepped out onto the veranda of the vicarage and collected their umbrellas, the sound of Reverend Olten's coughing could still be heard from inside the house over the rattle of rain on the roof. A sub-inspector and two constables with rifles were waiting outside. They set off single file down the path, Edwin Pearson leading the way to the cemetery. Nobody spoke as they walked along a stream of muddy water that trickled down the slate-lined drain. Their black umbrellas looked like bats' wings. It made Jim think of a funeral procession. Walking behind his mother, he noticed that in her rush to leave the house, she had forgotten to put on her stockings, an inch of pale skin showing beneath the lace hem of her black dress.

THREE

When they reached the church, Inspector Pearson stopped to wipe the sweat off his face. He took out his pipe and filled it with tobacco before setting it alight. His tanned cheeks were flushed pink and his glasses had steamed up. The freckled dome of his bald head was beaded with perspiration.

By now the rain had tapered off and the clouds parted for a few seconds. Jim could see all the way across the kidney-shaped lake. There were no boats on the water. Amongst the trees he could see houses scattered up the slopes on either shore all the way to Tallital. Whenever the mist cleared suddenly, as it did just now, revealing the forested slopes and the green expanse of still water, Jim imagined that the clouds had taken something away with them—landmarks washed away in a flood. Yet everything seemed to be there, even as he surveyed the rooftops to see which house or path might have disappeared. Jim felt sure that something was gone but he couldn't put his finger on what that might be.

Earlier that morning, he had climbed over the lower wall of the cemetery but this time Reverend Olten had given them the key and one of the constables unlocked the heavy brass padlock. Leading the way, Jim circled down to the left, past his father's headstone. Mary Jane paused a moment to brush aside the fallen deodar needles from the marble plaque. Christopher Corbett was her second husband. He had been the postmaster in Nainital. Twice widowed, Mary Jane was left with twelve children to raise on her own.

By the time they reached the terrace where Cindy Bertram's grave had been unearthed, Inspector Pearson was out of breath and his pipe had gone out. The rain had started again, sifting through

11

the branches. For several minutes nobody said anything, standing under their umbrellas and staring at the cavity in the ground where the broken coffin lay like the wreckage of a small wooden boat.

'Whoever did this must have taken the casket out and emptied it, then put it back, Sir,' the Sub-inspector said, pointing. 'See where they dragged it over there, near that other grave.'

Jim could clearly make out the marks of the coffin being slid through the mud. He noticed a splinter of wood had broken off. As they studied the area near the grave for any other evidence, Jim saw that his mother stood apart from the men, watching with a distraught expression on her face. Pearson and the others circled around, scanning the ground. Monsoon weeds had been crushed and they could see more footprints, at least one pair of shoes as well as bare feet.

'Here's something,' said one of the constables in Hindustani, pushing aside a clump of stinging nettle with his boot.

Half-hidden in the grass lay an empty bottle. Jim knew it must have contained whisky. There wasn't any cap on the bottle and he could see the yellowish dregs of liquor near the tapered neck where it rested on its side amidst the weeds, as if someone had taken a final swig then tossed it aside.

'Don't touch it,' Pearson said.

Just then, Mary Jane gave a startled cry. Wheeling around, Jim saw his mother balancing on one leg, holding her umbrella above her head like a trapeze artist.

'It's nothing,' she said, flustered, 'a leech, that's all.'

Jim could see blood on her ankle. He stepped around the grave and went across to where his mother stood. Mrs Corbett smiled at her son as if to reassure him, though her face looked ashen and drawn. The leech must have gorged itself and fallen off. A trickle of blood marked a trail from below the hem of his mother's black dress into the heel of her shoe. When Jim glanced towards the policemen, they turned away, embarrassed, as if they shouldn't have been staring.

'It's all right. Will you wipe it for me?' his mother said, passing Jim her handkerchief. 'I'll get a sticking plaster when we get home.'

Crouching, he dabbed at the blood on her leg. When he wiped the spot where the leech had fastened on he could see a small, dark welt. Immediately, the blood began to ooze again, trickling from his mother's ankle. Mixed with the rain, it fell as a single drop that disappeared into the moss at their feet.

As Jim looked down, he saw something lying amidst the ferns, six inches from his mother's shoe. The tiny object was no bigger than a pea. Its dull, yellow colour caught his eye. At first he thought it was a pebble. Reaching over, he picked it up. By this time, his mother had stepped aside, pressing her handkerchief against the leech bite to staunch the bleeding. As soon as Jim's fingers closed around the object, he knew exactly what it was and his nerves burned at the touch. A human molar, it had discoloured roots and a dented crown. Jim's fingers trembled so hard, he was afraid of dropping the tooth.

Nobody else had noticed what he'd found. Inspector Pearson and the other three men had moved off towards the cemetery gate. Mary Jane Corbett was staring in the opposite direction, beyond her husband's grave. The tooth looked like a misshapen pearl, decayed and stained. Jim was about to call out to the others but something made him stop, a sudden irrational impulse to keep this discovery to himself. Standing abruptly, he slipped the molar into the pocket of his shorts, as if it were a gruesome secret he needed to conceal and protect.

FOUR

Sunday morning, the four-note call of an Indian cuckoo made Jim glance up from the pages of *Great Expectations*. The heavy volume was part of a complete set of Charles Dickens' *Collected Works*, which had belonged to his father. It was one of the heaviest books in the house. Jim had read it last year and he enjoyed the story, though it made him wonder why anyone would want to live in London. Carefully placing a maidenhair fern between two sheets of newsprint he sandwiched it inside the book. Closing the covers, he stacked four other volumes on top for extra weight and shoved them to the back of the desk.

With everything that had happened the day before, Jim felt uneasy. He kept thinking of the shattered coffin and the Bible verse: '...whom shall I fear?'

After coming home from the cemetery the day before, he had gone to the godown at the back of Gurney House, where he kept his collections. It was a dark, airless room with a single window, used for storing wood and coal. He had taken over a corner and put in shelves, along with an old cupboard that his mother had removed from the kitchen. This was filled with bottles of snakes and other reptiles preserved in alcohol, cases of butterflies and beetles, lichens and mushrooms, stuffed birds and even a bat he'd skinned and mounted with its wings outstretched. The other half of his collection was in the family home in Kaladhungi, near Chhoti Haldwani, where he had amassed an assortment of creatures and plants from the bhabar and terai, including three cases of birds' eggs gathered from nests in the jungle. He had carefully labelled each specimen with its name, as well as the date and location where it was found.

From amongst the containers in which he stored his more precious objects, he had found an empty matchbox. Taking the tooth from his pocket, he had placed it there. The only light had come through the dusty windowpane but the molar glinted in the shadows, its enamel stained a dull yellow. Jim had hidden the tooth amongst his other relics.

Once again, the cuckoo's call chimed somewhere beyond the edge of the yard. Jim went out onto the veranda, the screen door clapping behind him. Nothing but mist lay outside. Jim couldn't even see the chicken wire fence. Inside the kitchen, he heard his sisters getting breakfast ready.

Jim imitated the cuckoo's call—a loud four-note whistle. After a few seconds, his call was answered: Ka...phal...pak...o! Kaphal pako! Here in Kumaon, the cuckoo's cry announced that wild kaphal berries were ripe. The birds began to call in May when the trees in the forest were laden with fruit. But now it was August, long past the season for kaphal berries or cuckoos. Jim went around the corner of the house, towards the path that came up from the lake. He squinted into the mist but all he could see were the moss-laden limbs of oaks by the gate. Cupping both hands around his mouth, he whistled once more.

This time the response was almost immediate, an instant echo. Ka...phal...pak o! At the same moment, Jim saw a familiar figure coming up the path. Emerging from the mist, the boy opened the gate. About Jim's age, he was dressed in a coarse woollen vest over a torn shirt and trousers. Gyan Chand's feet were bare and he carried a pair of milk cans on his back. His hair was damp and dishevelled. A wisp of a moustache darkened his upper lip. The two boys gave each other a casual salute.

'So, you've brought kaphal today?' Jim asked in Hindustani.

Gyani laughed, reaching over his shoulder into the rope bag that held the milk cans. He took out a dented oatmeal tin. Prying open the lid he showed Jim the contents.

'No...blackberries,' he said. 'Yesterday, the Missahib asked me to bring these. My sisters picked them.'

Together they went around to the back of the house and entered through the kitchen door. Jim's half-sister, Mary, the eldest, had a couple of kettles boiling on the wood-burning stove. She watched Gyani as he shrugged the rope bag off his shoulders. The milk cans were made of galvanized steel, their wooden stoppers sealed with a wadding of green leaves.

Mary took a pan from the shelf as Gyani measured out the milk.

'How much water have you added today?' she demanded. Jim knew that Mary was as gentle and generous as any woman could be, though she maintained a stern manner with servants and tradesmen.

Gyani grinned. 'Missahib, you should be asking me instead how much milk I've mixed with the water,' he said in a mischievous voice. 'There's a spring near our village that flows with cream.'

Mary frowned at him, though there was a smile in her eyes.

'I've brought the blackberries you asked for,' Gyani said, showing her the tin. Mary sniffed them. 'Picked fresh last evening.'

'How much do you want for them?' Mary asked.

'It doesn't matter. Whatever you wish, Missahib. My younger sisters picked these. I'll buy some sweets in town for them.'

Mary emptied the tin into an enamel bowl. The mass of blackberries looked almost alive, each of them ready to burst with juice. Jim knew that she would make a couple of pies this evening. Mary handed Gyani a one anna coin, which he slid into the inner pocket of his vest. She then poured out two glasses of tea for the boys from a pan brewing on the stove. Taking their tea outside, they squatted at the edge of the veranda. The two of them had known each other for three years, ever since Gyani began delivering milk after his father's leg was broken by one of their buffaloes. Jim had visited his village, Ransuri, which was five miles from Nainital on the other side of Sher ka Danda Ridge. Gyani did the walk every day, leaving home before dawn. His father, Umedh Chand had delivered milk to the Corbetts for almost twenty years.

'Have you heard?' Jim asked, taking a sip of tea.

'What?' said Gyani.

'One of the graves in the cemetery was dug up and the bones

were stolen. I found it yesterday morning...' Jim began, eyeing his friend. After that, he told the rest of the story—about the broken coffin, the bare footprints in the mud, and the empty whisky bottle. He was tempted to tell Gyani about the tooth but kept it to himself. The longer Cindy Bertram's molar lay in his possession the more difficult it became for him to confess the truth.

'Who would dig up a grave?' Gyani said, shaking his head. 'What would they have done with the bones?'

'I know, it makes no sense...' Jim took another swallow of the thick, sugary tea. Mary always added fresh ginger, the way he liked it.

'Maybe there wasn't a body,' Gyani said, after thinking a moment. 'Maybe something else was buried there.'

'That's not possible,' said Jim. 'My mother attended the funeral. She saw the coffin lowered into the ground.'

Gyani shrugged. 'Then it could be an evil spirit.'

Jim laughed and rolled his eyes. According to Gyani, the forests of Kumaon were full of ghosts and demons—bhoots, prets, churails. He claimed that the shadow of a stooped old witch wandered through the Tallital Bazaar in the middle of the night ringing a silver bell. Near the burning ghat in the valley, where Hindus cremated their dead, malevolent vampires, called vaital, roosted in the trees, hanging upside down like bats. One or two of the buildings in Nainital had resident phantoms, including the old Mission Hospital where an Irish nurse in a starched white uniform did her rounds at dusk, placing ice-cold hands on the foreheads of patients with fevers.

'It might be sadhus.' Gyani ran through all of the possibilities in his mind. He began to describe how Hindu mendicants collected ash and bones from cremation grounds and used these as ingredients for tantric rituals and sorcery. 'They crush the bones and make magic powders that give them supernatural powers.'

Jim shook his head. 'Rubbish,' he said.

'It's possible,' Gyani said, finishing the last of his tea.

Standing up, he hoisted the milk cans onto his shoulders. 'I have to go. Yesterday, Tanner Memsahib got angry with me because I delivered her milk five minutes late. You know how she can yell and shout!'

Mrs Tanner lived half a mile from Gurney House and she was known for her short temper. Jim had often been on the receiving end of her scoldings, most recently when he chased a wounded pheasant into her yard, just as she came outdoors to beat her carpets. He reminded his friend how she had shooed him off with a walking stick.

Gyani laughed as he stopped at the gate before opening the latch. 'It must have been a ghost,' he said, calling over his shoulder, 'a bhoot or vaital that disturbed her grave.'

Jim waved him away.

'Ghosts don't leave footprints!' he cried, though he sounded unconvinced.

FIVE

St John in the Wilderness Church was given its name by the Bishop of Calcutta, Daniel Wilson. He camped here in the forest above Nainital in 1844, before laying the cornerstone and consecrating the ground on which the sanctuary was built. The bell tower with its four spires made Jim think of Ivanhoe's castle. He liked to imagine what must have stood on this knoll before the stone walls went up. There would have been an open glade surrounded by oaks, rhododendron and anyar trees (*Lyonia ovalifolia*) with their poisonous leaves and pendant white blossoms. The deodars and cedars had been planted a few years later. Jim wished he could have seen Nainital before any settlement came up, a perfect, peaceable Eden, where animals drank at the lakeshore, before human inhabitants built temples and churches, houses and shops. Inside the church, he liked the stained-glass windows, though he hated the hard wooden pews and interminable sermons. The Corbetts, a dozen of them altogether, filed into the same pew, sitting in a compact row, with Mary Jane at one end and her eldest son, Tom, at the other. They were a musical family and led the hymns with a strong chorus of voices. Jim sat next to Maggie, who was older than him by a year, his favourite sister. He had a clear tenor voice, though it was changing now, his vocal chords betraying him on the high notes.

Jim had only a few memories of his father, who retired as postmaster at the mandatory age of fifty-five, and died of a weak heart two years later. He could recall Christopher Corbett sitting at the end of the pew but could not remember his voice, only a blurred memory of his kindly features and moist eyes behind a pair of spectacles. A few years ago, before he knew better, he had asked

Maggie if she thought their mother had loved their father more than her first husband, Charles Doyle. She had been married to Doyle at the age of fifteen and bore him three children, before he was killed in the 1857 Mutiny. Though a civilian, Doyle was given command of the Etawah Light Horse and died in action at the Battle of Harchandpore. Christopher Corbett, who was a quiet, bookish man, not a dashing cavalry officer, had also been married once before. When he and Mary Jane Doyle remarried at St Paul's Church in Landour, in 1859, they had three children each from their previous unions. Together they conceived six more, the eldest of whom was Tom and the youngest, Archibald D'Arcy. Jim (christened Edward James) was the second youngest, born in 1875.

Considering her brother's question thoughtfully, Maggie understood the soil out of which it had sprouted. Within a large family such as theirs, each of them had alliances and knew their place in the ladder of things. Love was a word they all used, though it suggested layers of endearment, as well as mysterious longings and unspoken desires. Jim had to wonder if his mother still grieved for Charles Doyle, or whether she had been happier in the arms of the soft-spoken postmaster who liked to read Dickens aloud to his children. After a while, Maggie answered him, saying she supposed 'Mother must have loved both husbands equally much in different ways.' It was a diplomatic reply, which had left Jim dissatisfied and confused.

By the time everyone gathered for the ten o'clock service, news of the empty grave had spread throughout the town. Jim knew that everyone in church was watching him. Inspector Pearson, who sat three pews ahead of theirs beside his wife, had taken Jim's statement the evening before and made him sign the document, witnessed by his mother and brother Tom.

With Reverend Olten still sick, the service was led by Reverend Samuel Newcomb, a missionary from Shikoabad, who was holidaying in Nainital. He was in his late thirties, with a shock of red hair and a crippled arm hidden beneath his robes. His shoulder twisted awkwardly when he moved, as if he were trying to reach for something but couldn't get his body to respond.

Today the invocation was longer than usual, which promised a protracted sermon. Reverend Newcomb put special emphasis on phrases like 'deliver us from the darkness of the tomb' and 'let our mortal flesh rise up and be purified by the radiance of thy love'. The New Testament reading was from the Gospel of John, Chapter 20, about the stone being rolled away from the tomb and the disappearance of Jesus's body.

As he began his homily, Reverend Newcomb reminded the congregation that 'our daughter, Cynthia, has been stolen from us'. He spoke about how Jesus had 'freed himself from the shackles of death and now walks amongst us as the risen Christ'. Jim squirmed in his seat, feeling the eyes of others upon him, as Maggie sat beside him with her hands folded in her lap. The preacher began to speak of the wilderness into which John the Baptist had wandered, how he wore the skins of animals and fed himself on the honey of wild bees. Though he didn't mention leopards, Reverend Newcomb spoke of 'dangerous and savage beasts, which can only be tamed by God'. Glancing down to the end of the pew, Jim could see his mother's stern profile facing straight ahead. He wondered if she had ever walked past a leopard in the dark without knowing it was there. Maybe his mother had been stalked by the same man-eater that killed Cindy Bertram. The idea tightened like a slip knot around his neck, as if his tie had shrunk.

Jim remembered the bare footprints in the mud and wondered again who might have unearthed the grave. He could picture a group of anonymous men digging in the darkness, their picks and spades gouging into the soil, the sound of metal striking something solid, voices whispering as they dragged the rotting coffin out of the ground, wrenching nails from the mouldering planks of wood.

'Our daughter's precious body was laid to rest in sacred ground. She knows only the joys of heaven, not the abomination of this earth. Don't be afraid for her, or for yourselves.' Reverend Newcomb threw up his right hand and the sleeve of his robe fell down to his shoulder, while the other arm hung limp at his side.

It had started raining once again and Jim could hear approaching thunder. He wondered what the grave robbers could have taken. Soon there was lightning outside, which lit up the stained-glass windows in bright flashes of colour.

Reverend Newcomb continued speaking, raising his voice over the gathering storm. 'The decay of our mortal remains is part of the degradation of this earth. Rejoice! Cynthia is with her saviour! God's own angels have lifted her up and taken her through the high gates of heaven. They have carried her home in their chariots. No one can harm her now. She is wearing a satin gown and singing hymns in paradise. She has been released from the horrors of this world and will live forever in the gentle arms of Jesus.'

Jim tried not to think about it but he kept picturing what was left of his father, decaying bones encased in the earth, along with the unfortunate victims of the great landslip. His mother still kept her husband's pocket watch on her dressing table and his wedding ring in a lacquer pillbox that also contained a lock of his grey hair tied with a black ribbon. She had mourned him for the past eight years. Like Queen Victoria, Mrs Corbett still wore her widow's weeds.

'The evildoers will rise up against us! They will mock our commandments and defile our graves...' Reverend Newcomb continued, his voice strangled by emotion. 'We must show them the light, even as they live in corruption and greed. The Lord will punish them. He will bring down his wrath and vengeance upon them. We must not fear, for the God of our fathers will protect us beyond the shadows of the grave. Those men who have violated the covenant of the Lord, who have disturbed the final resting place of the righteous, they will not escape judgment...'

By this time the rain was coming down so hard outside, it was impossible to hear the preacher even as his voice rose to challenge the elements. Jim glanced across at Maggie, who stifled a smile. Reverend Newcomb raised his good arm and began to pray, though the words were lost in the raging tumult of the storm. After that, they all rose to sing the last hymn. Jim and Maggie held the hymnal between them and let their voices rise above the monsoon gale.

With Christ we share a mystic grave,
With Christ we buried lie;
But 'tis not in the darksome cave
By mournful Calvary.

The pure and bright baptismal flood
Entombs our nature's stain;
New creatures from the cleansing wave
With Christ we rise again.

SIX

By Monday afternoon, two men had been arrested in connection with the desecration of Cynthia Bertram's grave. Both of them were day labourers working on a road gang for the PWD. They admitted to having been hired to dig up the coffin but said they had been cheated and received only half the money they were promised. The name of the person who hired them hadn't been released because the police were searching for him, though they expected to make an arrest within the next forty-eight hours.

Tom came home with this news when he and his wife, Emily, arrived at Gurney House in time for dinner. Having taken over his father's job as postmaster, he was often the first person to know what was happening in Nainital, since all of the mail and telegrams went through his office. Jim had always admired Tom who was a prize-winning marksman and accomplished shikari. Though it was close season now for hunting small and large game, they had a roast leg of wild boar for dinner. Tom had shot it two nights ago over a potato field northeast of town, along the Almora Cart Road. One of the farmers had complained that the boar were destroying his fields and Tom agreed to sit up and kill one. Classified as vermin, boar could be shot without a permit any time of year. Jim would have liked to have gone hunting with his brother but his mother had insisted that he stay home, for he had school the next day. With a dozen mouths to feed, the Corbett household depended on Tom and others to bring home meat for the pot. Jim was already making his contributions. During the winter holidays, when they moved down to the farm at Kaladhungi, he brought home wildfowl and venison two or three times a week.

'Where did they hide the bones?' Jim asked his brother.

'No idea,' said Tom, chewing slowly as he sat at the head of the table. 'The police aren't releasing any more information until the case is solved.'

'But was the skeleton intact?'

'No more questions, James,' his mother said from her end of the table. 'We're eating dinner and this isn't a conversation I choose to hear.'

Maggie looked across at him and smirked. The boar was tough and gamy, as meat always was in the monsoon. Tom had also brought a bag full of new potatoes from the farmer's field, where the boar had uprooted them.

As soon as the meal was over and the table had been cleared, Maggie and her sisters stood around the piano playing duets while Jim went out onto the veranda, where Tom was having a smoke on his own. The rain had stopped but the trees were dripping. Jim could see glow-worms in the flowerbeds.

'Did you know Cindy Bertram?' he asked his brother.

Tom blew out a ring of smoke, then exhaled the rest in a thin stream that passed through the centre like an arrow piercing its target. This was a trick Jim had always liked and there was enough lamplight coming through the drawing room window for him to see the smoke ring dispersing in the dark. Dozens of moths had collected on the glass panes, their wings silhouetted against the amber glow.

'Yes...not well, but I knew her. She was a couple years younger than me.'

'Did you see her body after she was found?' Jim asked.

The tip of Tom's cigarette glowed in the dark as he inhaled.

'We all helped carry her up,' his brother said. 'She was a long way down the khud in a steep nullah, surrounded by cliffs.' He described exactly where it was, a spot that Jim knew well, along the Kaladhungi Road, just beyond a burnt tree that had been struck by lightning.

'Are you sure it was a leopard that killed her?' Jim asked.

There was silence for almost a minute, in which he could hear the girls' voices and laughter inside and a few notes from the piano.

'Might have been,' said Tom at last. 'But I suppose we'll learn the truth once the police have cracked the case.'

Jim could tell that his brother knew more than he was willing to say, though Tom continued speaking.

'About a week after Cindy Bertram died, I shot a leopard near the spot where she was found, lower down the Kaladhungi Road. Most people believed it was the same animal that killed Cindy. Afterwards, no more attacks occurred, so it could have been. But I've never been sure,' said Tom.

A bat was flying over their heads, feeding on moths drawn to the light from indoors. Jim could see only a shadow where his eldest brother sat and the flickering ember of his cigarette.

'Most man-eaters are old or crippled,' said Tom, 'that's why they start killing people. Human beings are easier to stalk than deer. But the leopard I shot was in her prime, a healthy young female. When I skinned her, I cut open her stomach to see what she'd eaten, in case there were human remains. But the last meal she'd had was a langur. I also discovered she was carrying two cubs in her womb.'

Jim could picture the pained expression on his brother's face. Tom had a sensitive nature and Jim had seen him cry more than once, at little things that didn't seem to matter. During their father's funeral, Tom had broken down. Even his sisters were stronger than him and held their grief within themselves. Jim had always idolized his brother, though he knew his weaknesses as if they were his own.

'Are those the pair of cubs you gave me?' Jim asked.

'Yes, they are,' Tom said, flicking the fag end of his cigarette out onto the lawn. 'The same ones.'

'If she wasn't killed by a man-eater,' Jim said, 'then how did Cindy die?'

Tom got to his feet and stretched, ready to take his wife home. She was expecting their first child.

'It wasn't an accident, that's for sure,' Tom said in an offhand way. 'And Cindy Bertram wasn't an innocent victim, if you know what I mean...'

Jim didn't understand but before he could ask any more questions the screen door slammed shut and his brother had gone back into the house. Following him, Jim got a candle stub from the kitchen and carried it out to the godown. In the darkness, he fumbled with the latch and finally got it open. Striking a match, he lit the candle and set it on top of the cupboard. From a shelf, he took down a wide-mouthed bottle with a cork stopper sealed with wax. The smell of formaldehyde was overpowering. Holding the bottle near the candle flame, he dusted off the glass and studied what lay inside. Two unborn leopard cubs floated in the bottle. They were facing each other and their umbilical cords were coiled around them like worms. The tiny feline faces were pinched and the eyes were shut but he could just make out the faint pattern of rosettes on their fur and the round pads of their paws. The cubs were six inches long but fully formed. In the glimmering light of the candle flame, Jim could almost imagine them coming back to life. Tom had given him these specimens two years ago from his collection, most of which he had destroyed or discarded when he got married and moved into his own house.

Putting the bottle back on the shelf, Jim rummaged about among the matchboxes until he found the one containing Cindy Bertram's tooth. He opened it slowly and held it close to the light. This time he did not touch it. For a moment this evening, he had almost told Tom what he'd found but each of them had their own secrets to keep.

Behind a stack of biscuit tins that contained an assortment of snakeskins and wild silk cocoons, he located a hidden packet of cigarettes. Taking one out and tapping it on the back of his hand the same way Tom tamped his cigarettes, Jim leaned towards the burning candle and lit up. Then blowing out the flame, he pinched the wick. In the musty darkness, the tobacco smoke was invisible, though Jim smelled its roasted fragrance and felt the fumes enter his lungs like a vaporous spirit seeking refuge from the night.

SEVEN

Neville Terrance Murchison looked much older than his thirty-four years. He was one of the poorest whites in Nainital, without a home to call his own and no family that would claim him. Most of the time he slept in a cowshed to the east of town, along the shortcut to Jeolikot. Occasionally, he would get himself washed and shaved and show up in church, or on the parade ground for the Queen's birthday, though hardly anyone acknowledged his existence. Over the years, he had held a few jobs but never for more than a couple of months. The longest he'd worked in one place was as a marker at Raymond's Hotel, where he played lawn tennis with those who didn't have partners and kept the courts free of leaves and worms.

As a white man, he was allowed to walk along the Upper Mall Road, despite being an alcoholic with more debts than holes in his socks. Neville had been a handsome young man in his twenties and many people remembered him as a good dancer. But drink and opium had destroyed him as surely as the judgement of his peers. While the British authorities in India spoke disapprovingly of the Hindu caste system, blaming it for everything from native indolence to the fatalistic subservience of untouchable communities, the Raj had its own caste system, as rigidly enforced and ruthlessly codified as the Laws of Manu. 'Murch', as most people called him, was a victim of his own society. Like the Corbetts, he was a third generation white, or 'domiciled European', born in India, which placed him on the lower rungs of the ladder, just above the near-whites or Eurasians, chee-chees, as they were often called. Of course, plenty of Indians lay beneath them but they played their own games of snakes and ladders. 'Country-born' was a common expression. 'Country-bottled' was more often the euphemism. While the ingredients had come from England the final product was mixed up here, along with the adulteration this implied.

Murch had played tennis with high court judges and the wives of district collectors, even the Commissioner of Kumaon. He knew how to let them win, deftly placing his shots outside the lines when it came to match point. And he could dance a nimble quadrille or a foxtrot as well as anyone straight off the boat. Ultimately, though, he couldn't shut out the whispers—'nearly-native…the bugger talks Hindustani without an accent, swearing like a sepoy in three dialects'. It hurt him badly that though his game could be as graceful as any man who raised a racket and his tennis whites as bleached and perfectly creased as the napery at the Gurkha officers' mess, they dismissed him nonetheless, putting him down because of his place of birth.

Later, when he worked at another hotel in town, waiting tables, he would cringe when other country-borns tipped him a couple of annas but gladly spent it on home-brewed liquor, the sour katchee that he bought in the back lanes of Tallital Bazaar. More than once, Murch had to be removed from the Upper Mall for disorderly behaviour and inebriation but he was never banished completely because that would have been an admission that white men were beyond redemption. The town fathers tried to persuade him to mend his ways and good Christians prayed for his soul but Neville Terrance Murchison was already lost to his community. In the winter season, when most of the town shut down, he walked to Kathgodam and got odd jobs working for one of the European families that owned farms and orchards at the foot of the hill. He was not a hunter, but told good yarns, especially after a peg or two of Shahjahanpur rum. In the jungle, away from the rules and regulations of hill station life, people still found him entertaining. Eventually, Murch had disappeared for a couple of years and was rumoured to have gone off to work on an indigo plantation but he reappeared again with the same dissolute swagger, looking more desperate than ever.

Jim and his classmates at school had been warned about Murch.

This was what happened to men who drank with the natives. It wasn't clear which of the two was more dangerous—the alcohol consumed or the company you kept. In the last few years, Murch had also discovered the fatal pleasures of the poppy, which was being grown throughout the terai. Though he never gave up the bottle, the opium pipe had its own allure and offered a sounder, dreamless sleep. Once, when walking on the Upper Mall with his mother and sisters, Jim had seen Murch slumped on one of the wrought iron benches installed by the municipality, overlooking the lake. His eyes were glazed and he had called out in a cheerful voice, 'Good evening, ladies! May I have this dance?' Mary Jane Corbett moved quickly past, shepherding her daughters and ignoring the remark, though Jim had glanced back over his shoulder to see Murch rise to his feet and take a phantom partner in his arms, wheeling her around and around before spinning her off into the lake.

When he saw him now, Jim hardly recognized the man. The gaunt features were drawn and unshaven as he stood in the dock, wearing a soiled shirt and trousers and a pair of boots that looked as if they'd been discarded more than once. From thirty feet away, Jim could smell him too, the rank odours of a cowshed and unwashed human flesh. His hair had turned grey and fell to his shoulders. Most of his teeth had fallen out and his hands trembled as the magistrate asked him to state his name and the clerk wrote it down in the court ledger.

Inspector Pearson stood a few feet away, wiping perspiration from his bald head but with a satisfied look on his face, having got his man. He even winked at Jim, who sat between his mother and Tom. The Corbetts were country-bottled too, but they had manners and self-esteem that kept them afloat in Nainital. As people liked to say, there are only two things you can do in a lake, either you sink or you learn how to swim. Edward James Corbett already understood the hierarchies at work, the patronizing stare of the magistrate as he asked him what he'd found in the cemetery on Saturday morning, a week ago.

'How many footprints would you say there were?'

'At least three different sets of feet, sir,' he said. 'One with shoes and the other two of them bare.'

'If they were barefoot, how could you tell them apart?' the magistrate asked.

'Yes, sir. I mean, no…your honour,' he'd fumbled for a moment and looked across at Tom, then answered. 'One print was much longer, sir, and the other shorter and flatter and the right foot had only three toes.'

The magistrate raised an eyebrow and looked at Pearson, who nodded with satisfaction. 'The boy's right, your honour. One of the two coolies we arrested was missing two digits on his right foot.'

'You're an observant lad, Master Corbett,' the magistrate said. 'And what do you plan to become when you grow up?'

Jim stood a little taller now, his cap held in both hands. 'A tracker, sir. Like Hawk Eye in *The Pathfinder*, your honour.'

The magistrate looked baffled and Jim could almost hear his mother saying, 'That's enough, James.' Fortunately, the Inspector intervened.

'I believe it's an American novel, your honour. By James Fenimore Cooper. Very popular these days amongst the boys in school.'

'Aha, the Wild West!' said the magistrate. 'So, you're planning to head off there once you've had enough of the East.' Everyone in the courtroom laughed politely at the magistrate's attempted humour, except for Murch, who sat shivering in his chair between two constables. Whether it was malaria or delirium tremens nobody could be sure. He had pleaded not guilty to the charges of digging up Cindy Bertram's grave and when he was asked where he'd hidden her remains, he mumbled something about knowing 'nothing about any such thing'.

The magistrate dismissed Jim and banged his gavel, announcing that a trial would be scheduled within a fortnight. Until such time, the prisoner was to be housed in the police lock-up without recourse to bail, being indigent and more than likely to run away.

EIGHT

Many years later, Jim would write about his youthful experiences in the forests of Kumaon. His bestselling books describe how he learned the language of animals, their vocal range of alarm cries and mating calls, as well as the everyday chatter of birds and mammals going about the mundane business of feeding themselves and their young. More than anyone else, Corbett had an innate appreciation for the rich diversity of the Indian jungles, the multitude of species from paradise flycatchers to tigers, porcupines and elephants. His education in jungle lore began at an early age, both in Nainital and at Kaladhungi, fifteen miles walk apart, with a difference in altitude of four thousand feet. This trek between the Corbetts' summer and winter homes taught him how species vary from one elevation to another, along with seasonal changes in behaviour, plumage and diet. But most of all, he learned not to be afraid in the forest, neither during the day nor at night.

At the beginning of his first book, *Man-eaters of Kumaon*, he wrote:

When I see the expression 'cruel as a tiger' and 'as bloodthirsty as a tiger' in print, I think of a small boy armed with an old muzzle-loading gun—the right barrel of which was split for six inches of its length, and the stock and barrels of which were kept from falling apart by lashings of brass wire—wandering through the jungles of the terai and bhabar in the days when there were ten tigers to every one that now survives; sleeping anywhere he happened to be when night came on, with a small fire to give him company and warmth, wakened at intervals by the calling of tigers, sometimes in the distance, at other times near at hand; throwing another stick on the fire and turning over and continuing his interrupted sleep without one thought of unease; knowing from his own short experience and from what others, who like him had spent their days in the jungles, had told him, that a tiger, unless molested, would do him no harm; or during daylight hours avoiding any tiger he saw, and when that was not possible, standing perfectly still until it had passed and gone, before continuing on his way. And I think of him on one occasion stalking half-a-dozen junglefowl that were feeding in the open, and on creeping up to a plum bush and standing up to peer over, the bush heaving and a tiger walking out on the far side and, on clearing the bush, turning round and looking at the boy with an expression on its face which said as clearly as any words, 'Hello, kid, what the hell are you doing here?' and receiving no answer, turning round and walking away very slowly without once looking back.

After he became a celebrated hunter and naturalist, Corbett was awarded 'freedom of the forests' by the British government in India, though he had already enjoyed that freedom as a boy. His mother and sisters were protective of him in other ways but they allowed him to roam at will, either on his own or accompanied by Kunwar Singh, one of their neighbours in Kaladhungi. Tom, his eldest brother, initiated him in the sport of hunting, its rules and rituals. The jungles taught him independence from an early age. Firearms weren't heavily regulated. Corbett describes how, as the youngest cadet in the Nainital Voluntary Rifles, at the age of ten, he was given a lesson in marksmanship by a visiting officer who went on to become Field Marshal Earl Roberts, the hero of Kandahar. On the Sukha Tal firing range, he aimed a heavy .450 Martini rifle and hit a target at 200 yards four out of five times. The recoil bruised his shoulder but, as a reward, the sergeant major allowed Jim to take the rifle home with him during his winter holidays, along with as much ammunition as he required.

That winter, he shot his first leopard and was nearly killed in the process when the wounded animal leapt directly over his head, spattering his clothes with blood. Though he was enormously proud of this trophy, Corbett seldom killed animals gratuitously. In later years, he traded his gun for a camera, becoming one of the first wildlife photographers in India. His proudest accomplishment was calling seven tigers together and capturing them on film.

All of this can be found in his books. Most readers are familiar with Jim Corbett, the white hunter, who rid the forests of the Lower Himalayas of man-eating tigers and leopards that terrorized villagers and claimed thousands of victims. Nevertheless, at the age of fourteen, Jim had just begun to understand that the most dangerous creature on earth is man. Having seen the shivering, desperate figure of Murch produced in court, he realized that human depravity and evil are more than just admonitions from the Scriptures, rather they are things that live and breathe among us.

The jungle, with its wildlife and beauty, represented the primal purity of nature, while human beings possessed a different kind of savagery.

NINE

A fortnight is a long time to wait. Murch refused to confess and the police had no luck tracing Cindy Bertram's remains. Speculation and rumours ran wild in Nainital. There were some who believed the bones had been sold to Amroha hakims, who concocted occult remedies from gruesome ingredients. Others were convinced it was a posthumous act of revenge kindled by a failed love affair. Though she had died more than ten years ago, plenty of people in Nainital remembered that Cindy had been an attractive, flirtatious girl pursued by most of the bachelors in town. Several hearts had been broken and she was briefly engaged to three different men over the course of a single summer season. She liked to dance and enjoyed the attention of young soldiers and civil servants, even a visiting viscount, who was a nephew of the queen. Though it was considered wrong to speak ill of the dead, there were many who claimed she had fallen for Murch when he was still a handsome, charming young man. From the same social strata, they would have made an acceptable couple, though a young girl with good looks always had prospects of marrying above her class.

At school, Jim was teased mercilessly for having discovered the empty grave. Several of the older boys accused him of digging it up himself and called him a ghoul. They mocked him for collecting ferns and sniggered behind his back. 'Whose grave d'you rob today?' he was asked. 'Oy, Corbett, I've got some nice rotten bones for your lunch.' It wasn't easy but he ignored the remarks, knowing that if he answered back it would only get worse. Even a couple of the teachers gave him a hard time, suggesting 'Master Corbett might share some insights on the afterlife'. In the end, he finally lost his temper with a classmate, Toby Duggan, who asked him if he'd picked the ferns for a girlfriend. During recess, Jim tackled Duggan, the two of them rolling about in the dust until one of the teachers pulled them apart. The Principal's solution to the conflict was to send for two pairs of boxing gloves and set the combatants upon each other again, refereeing the fight himself. By this time, Jim's anger had diminished and he felt foolish wearing the heavy gloves filled with coconut fibres. He swung at his opponent a couple of times as a ring of jeering boys surrounded them, demanding honour and blood. Eventually, in the third round, Jim landed a right hook and watched bewildered as Duggan staggered backwards and fell to the ground.

When he got home, Maggie was the first to notice his black eye. Jim's mother scolded him for fighting, though she knew better than to demand more of an explanation than he was willing to give. The next day he skipped school and took off early in the morning, setting out along the Upper Kaladhungi Road before first light. He knew this route so well he could have walked it blindfolded. By the time he reached the third bend, beyond the burnt tree that Tom had described, there was enough light for him to see all the way down the khud. Being monsoon, every spring was spewing from the rocks, as if the mountains had sprung hundreds of leaks. He was below the clouds by now and the air was warmer. Jim hadn't brought a gun, for his muzzle-loader was covered in grease and wrapped in an oilcloth to protect it from the corrosive humidity of the rains.

Climbing hand over hand down a retaining wall, he jumped the last six feet onto a narrow ledge that offered access to the ravine. If there was a path, it was completely overgrown and Jim couldn't find it. He felt sure he would step on a snake, the only creature he feared. But after a ways, it was easier going and he was able to skid down the slope and reach the bottom. He remembered how his brother had said it took more than a dozen men to bring the body up. There were cliffs on either side. The watercourse, which would have been dry in April when Cindy died, was filled by a good-sized stream this time of year, cascading over rocks and boulders. He tried to imagine a leopard carrying its human victim down this khud and wondered why it would have chosen such a precipitous place. After fifty yards, he came to a waterfall, which Tom had told him about and, below that, a dense thicket of brambles and burrs. This was the spot. No doubt about it. Jim felt an itch at the back of his neck.

He wasn't completely sure why he had come here but it seemed as if he might discover an answer to questions that hadn't yet formed in his mind. Tom's words still stuck in Jim's memory... 'Cindy Bertram wasn't an innocent victim, if you know what I mean.' It was obvious that nobody had been here recently and he felt like a detective visiting the scene of a forgotten crime, though there was nothing but forest all around and no reason to believe any violent acts had occurred down this khud.

The day before, Jim had brought the corked bottle out of the godown and studied the pair of leopard cubs in clear daylight. The fluid had grown cloudy and the specimens had a soapy whiteness like wax. He could imagine them curled up inside their mother's womb, surrounded by amniotic fluids instead of formaldehyde, possessed of a wild innocence in their unborn state. At the same time there was something disturbing about the specimens, a pickled vision of the grotesque.

The khud was the wrong sort of place to hide a kill, too close to the Kaladhungi Road. Beyond the thicket lay another waterfall, a hundred-foot drop. There was only one way in and out of the gorge. Jim could identify most of the plants and trees growing in the ravine where Tom had told him the body was found. After satisfying himself, he climbed out of the valley and back onto the road, picking burrs and leeches off his socks.

As soon as he got home, he went to the writing desk in the drawing room and tore a sheet of paper from the back of a copybook. In a neat, careful hand, with the formality he felt his observations deserved, Jim wrote them down for Inspector Pearson. After he finished, he added a title and his name:

Edward James Corbett

Observations on the Site where
Cynthia Bertram's Body was Found

1. The location of the body was 200 yards below the point where the Upper and Lower Kaladhungi Roads meet. If a leopard killed Cynthia Bertram on the lakeshore near Smuggler's Rock where she was last seen, the man-eater would have had to pass through a heavily settled area, crossing the Abbey and Dalhousie Estates, and covering a total distance in excess of three miles. Logically, it should have carried its kill into the denser, less inhabited jungles of Anyarphatta instead, only half a mile away and directly above Smuggler's Rock.

2. The khud in which the body was found is very steep on all sides, with a waterfall at one end. A leopard is unlikely to have chosen this spot, for it offers no means of escape. Leopards are cautious animals and always leave room for retreat.

3. The only access to the ravine is straight down a 40-foot pushta built between two limestone cliffs. A leopard carrying a body weighing more than 100 pounds could not have negotiated this approach. However, it would have been easy enough for someone to throw the corpse from above and let it roll all the way down to the bottom.

4. The area where the body was found is overgrown with cockle burrs, which most animals avoid, especially those with fur to which they adhere.

TEN

Nainital takes its name from a Hindu myth. The goddess immolates herself because her father has insulted her husband, Lord Shiva, creator and destroyer of the universe. When Shiva discovers what his consort has done, he is so distraught that he picks up her partially burned corpse and wanders across the land, from the Himalayas to the sea, in an apocalyptic fit of rage and mourning. Charred body parts are scattered at different places all across India. These sites are now revered as sacred centres of worship. 'Naina' refers to the eyes of the goddess, which fell by this secluded lake. A temple that stands on its shore is dedicated to the goddess, Naina Devi. The horrific tragedy of the myth and Lord Shiva's terrifying grief seem worlds away from the placid waters and verdant forests of Kumaon.

More recently, this lake was said to have been 'discovered' by an English sugar merchant and sportsman, Peter Barron, who stumbled upon the idyllic spot while on a shooting ramble in the Lower Himalayas. By then, the region had come under the control of British authorities following the Gurkha Wars, in 1816. The hill station of Nainital was founded as a European settlement in 1841.

Jim knew the history and lore of his birthplace, both the colonial stories and Hindu myths, but for him the natural history was far more compelling. From as long ago as he could remember, he had memorized the names of plants and insects, birds and mammals. Painted Jezebel butterflies, pygmy owlets, pangolins or strangler figs captured his imagination more than supernatural myths or heroic tales of conquest and discovery. From childhood, he spoke Hindustani with the same fluency as English and could identify species in either language.

His favourite pastime in Nainital was to go fishing in the lake.

Jim made his own bamboo rods out of stout ringal to catch the mighty mahseer, a native fish that fought more bravely and resolutely than a trout. He knew where the biggest mahseer could be found in secluded coves, near submerged trees. Maggie often accompanied him, and they would set off before breakfast to watch the sun rise over the shimmering surface of the lake. Often they would sit together on a rock and say nothing for an hour or two, waiting for a strike. At other times, they talked quietly, sharing confidences, idle thoughts and daydreams.

'Do you think they'll call you as a witness in the trial?' Maggie asked.

'I suppose,' said Jim, baiting the hook with a ball of dough to which he'd added a pinch of hing, or asafoetida, a secret he'd learned from a Mohammedan fisherman who had come up to the hills from Gorakhpur. He then cast it out as far as he could. The float was his own invention, fashioned from a porcupine quill.

'Murch is obviously guilty, isn't he?' Maggie said, once Jim had settled down beside her.

'The two coolies identified him as the one who hired them. It's their word against his,' said Jim. 'But they're locked up as well and might say anything to save their own skins.'

'Was he in love with her, do you think?' Maggie asked.

'Who? Cindy Bertram?'

'That's what they're saying. Murch loved her so terribly, he had her corpse dug up.' Maggie spoke in a whisper.

'Not a very romantic thing to do,' said Jim, reaching into his rucksack and taking out a packet of cigarettes. He offered one to Maggie but she shook her head and sat quietly as he lit the tobacco with a match.

'They say he's lost his mind, from drink and opium.'

'Murch looks like a lunatic, that's for sure,' said Jim, blowing out smoke rings warped by the breeze. It was still early, another half hour until dawn, and there was mist over the water. 'He might even believe he could raise her from the dead.'

Maggie fell silent for a while. She was a slender, athletic girl with sharp, inquisitive eyes. Though a year older than Jim, she could have been his twin, for they had the same delicate, determined features. Maggie wore a long skirt and a thick cotton blouse buttoned up to her neck, but this didn't stop her from keeping pace with Jim on the rocky paths, or scrambling down the khud.

'I saw a picture of Cindy Bertram the other day,' Maggie said. 'One of the girls at school found it in an album. She looked very pretty, dressed up for a Shakespearean tableau, playing Ophelia in *Hamlet*. She had a daisy crown on her head and wore a white muslin gown. There was an older man playing the ghost, and a lot of people I couldn't recognize but Tom was in it too, looking very handsome as Laertes, carrying a sword. We couldn't recognize Hamlet, though he certainly looked like a prince with a skull in his hand.'

'Tom said Cindy Bertram was two years younger than him,' said Jim.

'What else did he say?'

'Not much,' said Jim. 'Except that she wasn't an innocent victim... those were his words.'

Maggie plucked a stem of grass. 'What does that mean?'

'It wasn't a leopard that killed her,' Jim said.

'I've heard that too. They say she was murdered. But how was the poor girl to blame?' Maggie said.

'No idea,' said Jim. 'Maybe she made someone jealous.'

'Murch?'

'I suppose if you killed someone you loved, it might drive you crazy.' Jim tapped the ash from his cigarette and took a deep puff.

'But how can you love a person so much that you'd kill them? It doesn't make sense,' Maggie said.

'I wouldn't know,' said Jim. 'I've never been in love.'

His sister laughed. 'You had a crush on Mabel Fields.'

Jim reddened for a moment, then shook his head.

'Not any more. I don't have time for girls.'

Maggie took the cigarette from his hand and inhaled lightly, then gave it back.

Smoke streamed out of her lips with the words. 'I suppose some day I'll fall in love but hopefully not madly enough to kill someone.'

'That only happens in novels,' Jim said. 'You've been reading too many.'

'I heard something else,' said Maggie, looking at him out of the corner of her eye. 'Last night I was listening to Mother and Mary talking. They thought I'd fallen asleep and they were whispering between themselves. You know how Mother doesn't like gossip but she said she'd heard Cindy Bertram was pregnant when she died.'

Jim stubbed out the cigarette in the wet moss near his foot.

'How did she know?' he asked.

'Mother said she learned about it afterwards, from Mrs Jenson. Mary asked her if she knew who the father might have been but Mother said no, she wasn't sure.'

'That still doesn't explain anything, does it?' Jim said. 'I mean about the grave being dug up, or her death.'

'I suppose, somehow, it all fits together,' said Maggie.

'I keep thinking there has to be a simple, obvious answer,' Jim replied. 'On the surface it seems complicated but underneath the whole thing has got to make sense.'

'It's bobbing...' said Maggie softly.

'What?' he asked, distracted.

'There's a fish,' she said, nudging his arm.

Jim could see the porcupine quill dip under water and at the same moment, he set the hook with a sharp tug of the rod. He could feel the weight of the mahseer at the other end of the line and knew it would put up a good fight. The braided line began to sing as the fish ran off with the bait. He was using an old reel with a broken crank and tried to maintain tension with his thumb but the line cut him badly, drawing blood. Jim waited until the fish finally stopped before he began to retrieve the line, keeping the rod tip raised. Maggie was now on her feet as well and it took Jim ten minutes to land the fish. Typically, a mahseer fights a minute per pound and when he finally lifted the fish out of the water, he knew that was an accurate calculation of its weight. By now, the sun was just coming up over the rooftops of Tallital, and they set off for home along a shortcut that angled up the hill.

ELEVEN

By the time Jim and Maggie got home, Gyani had just arrived at Gurney House to deliver milk. He admired the fish, watching as Jim gutted it and removed the scales at the tap stand in the back garden. It was messy work. The guts and air sac were flung over the edge of the yard, where Jim knew the pine martens would find them, or maybe the jungle crows, whichever scavenger got there first. He used his skinning knife to clean the fish and cut off the head and tail, so it was ready for his sisters to cook up in a curry tonight. Then, washing his hands at the tap, he carried the fish inside before coming back out with two glasses of tea.

'I didn't know there were fish that size in the lake,' said Gyani.

'There are bigger ones than that,' said Jim. 'Near the Naina Devi temple I've seen a couple of huge mahseer, at least thirty pounds. The pandits feed them puffed rice and you can see them roll over on the surface.'

Gyani slurped his tea. 'I heard they arrested some men for digging up the grave.'

Jim nodded.

'One of them is an Englishman?' Gyani asked.

'Yes,' said Jim. 'A drunkard named Murchison.'

'Why would he have done it?'

'Nobody knows and he hasn't admitted to it yet.'

'The two other men who were arrested. They say they were beaten badly.' Gyani spoke softly. 'The police know how to get the truth out of you, one way or the other, usually with a cane. But they wouldn't beat an Englishman, would they?'

Jim looked aside and flicked a fish scale off his shorts. He took a swallow of tea before replying.

'The police are just doing their job. It's a dirty business…'

Gyani nodded.

'Last year there was a robbery at the Wellesley Girls' School, where I used to deliver milk to one of the teachers. The police stopped me and accused me of breaking in. I told them, "Sir, I'm a poor, honest boy. What would I steal?" They threatened me with their canes and abused me with language I can't repeat. But I was lucky…two other men from our village were delivering potatoes and they were taken to the lock-up where the police flogged them with a belt across the back of their legs. That way, the bruises don't show but it hurts so much a man will admit to crimes he'd never commit.'

'Couldn't they file a complaint?'

Gyani laughed. 'Nobody listens to poor farmers like us. We bring our milk and vegetables to town but then we go back home, disappearing into the jungle. For us, this is a foreign land. We don't belong here. We can't set foot on the Upper Mall Road without being arrested. For you sahib log, it's different.'

Jim had never heard Gyani speak with such bitterness and it surprised him, though he understood the emotions behind the words. While he could sit here and drink tea with Gyani, speaking casually in Hindustani, he knew that if some of the other whites in town had seen them, they would have objected. The separation between Indians and Europeans was ingrained in Nainital. He knew where the boundaries lay, those invisible lines that kept them apart, even if he transgressed those barriers. Jim also understood that Gyani faced discrimination from his own people because he was an untouchable, bearing the stigma of being an outcaste. They had never spoken about it but both of them understood the cruel inequities of the world in which they lived.

Jim considered Gyani his friend. They had hunted together and he had spent nights in his home, swapping stories around the clay hearth. Yet he wondered if Gyani thought of it as friendship, or something else. They finished their tea in silence but before he got up to leave, Gyani spoke again.

'I know you aren't like most of the sahibs,' said Gyani, 'and our family has eaten your family's salt for twenty years, before either of us was born…'

'Why are you talking like this?' Jim interrupted. 'Have I said something that offended you?'

'No,' Gyani shook his head. 'But, forgive me, I want to be sure I can trust you.'

'Of course, you can,' said Jim.

'If I were to tell you something…' Gyani's voice broke off. 'Would you go to the police?'

'It depends what it is,' Jim said, tossing the dregs of his tea in the grass.

'Or if you told the police, would you say that it came from me?' Gyani insisted. 'I need you to promise me this.'

'What do you want me to promise?' Jim said, confused.

'I want you to swear that if I tell you something,' said Gyani, 'the police must never find out that it came from me.'

Jim thought for a moment, knowing that Gyani was afraid. He was asking for proof of their friendship, an oath of trust.

'All right,' said Jim. 'I won't tell anyone you told me, whatever it might be.'

Gyani picked at a scab on his arm, then let out his breath as if he were about to jump off a cliff.

'I know where they took the bones,' he said.

Jim stared at him in alarm.

'They burned what was left of the body in the streambed, beyond the fallow fields across from our village, near the abandoned watermill where you and I shot a kakar last year. Remember? But further down in the valley where nobody goes.'

Gyani turned away as if he didn't want to look at Jim.

'How did you discover this?'

'I had gone to cut some timru twigs because my mother had a toothache. Last year when we were hunting there, I'd seen timru bushes growing below the mill, along the opposite slope of the valley. I had to climb down into the streambed to reach the other side. That's when I found the remains of the pyre. There wasn't much there, a few bits of charred wood and ashes. At first I thought someone had spent the night and lit a fire, but then I looked closer and I could see scraps of bones. A body had been cremated in secret, and that's when I understood…'

His eyes met Jim's and fear smouldered in his gaze.

'This was two days ago. I wasn't going to tell anyone,' he continued. 'If I went to the police, they would lock me up and accuse me of being one of the men who dug up the corpse. That's why I made you promise not to involve my name in this. You're the only person I can trust.'

Hearing the troubled emotions in Gyani's voice, Jim realized that he himself was being drawn into a knotted web of truth and lies. By accident, he had found the empty grave and could easily have walked away that morning, letting someone else discover the shattered coffin. Not only had he reported it, but then he had pocketed the tooth and kept it to himself, as if he shared the guilt for Cindy Bertram's death and the desecration of her corpse. In a sense, all of them were part of it, not just Murch or the two men he hired. Everyone in Nainital was guilty in some way, trapped in the shadows between right and wrong.

'Will you keep your promise?' Gyani said.

Jim nodded: 'Of course.'

TWELVE

News about the mystery of Cynthia Bertram's grave soon spread beyond Nainital to other parts of India. A week after the incident, *The Pioneer* newspaper, published in Allahabad, printed an article by a young assistant editor who was short on facts but well supplied with hyperbole:

IF TOMBSTONES COULD SPEAK!

Residents of Nainital are distressed by a strange event that occurred in the cemetery of St John in the Wilderness Church. The grave of a young woman, Cynthia Lily Bertram, who died ten years ago, has been unearthed and the body was found to have disappeared. Police are investigating and several arrests have been made but the motives behind this macabre crime remain unclear.

It is a sad day, when even the dead are not permitted to lie in peace. The European population in India suffers many hardships. Daily, they sacrifice the gentle comforts of home to serve Her Majesty's empire abroad. It is the white man's accepted burden that he should be shipped off to live in hostile, unhealthy conditions for the betterment of those poor, ignorant souls over whom Britannia casts her benevolent cloak. Malaria, cholera, dacoits, snakebite and thugs have all claimed their victims here in this ungrateful land. Those who are unfortunate enough to sacrifice their lives for India's good, must suffer the added indignity of being buried in foreign soil, leaving their loved ones bereaved and bereft.

One is reminded of Wordsworth's 'Elegiac Stanzas', of which

we quote but one:

Lamented Youth! to thy cold clay
Fit obsequies the Stranger paid;
And piety shall guard the Stone
Which hath not left the spot unknown
Where the wild waves resigned their prey—
And 'that' which marks thy bed.

By some accounts, the dreadful disinterment of this grave can be chalked up to native mischief. Certain Hindus, and some Mussalmans as well, are said to use the mortal remains of chaste victims for evil sorcery, grinding up human bones with mortar and pestle, to be served as balm for superstition and blind faith. If the police should discover that this is the work of a nefarious fakir they should spare no Christian forgiveness on the perpetrator. One of England's virgins, a fair daughter of our far-flung dominions in the East, has been denied her final, holy rest and is defiled by wanton greed and savage depravity.

Rudyard Kipling

Tom had brought a copy of *The Pioneer* home from the post office and Jim read the piece with consternation. He knew that tempers were rising in the town. Some of the boys at school were saying that they should go across to the police lock-up and 'horsewhip old Murch and those damned coolies, until they confessed'. He knew that if he told the police about the remains of the pyre Gyani had found, suspicion would immediately fall on the Hindu population and it was possible there might be reprisals.

He decided that he would go and take a look himself but had to wait until after church on Sunday morning. Meanwhile, Tom reported that a letter had arrived from Colleen Bertram, Cindy's mother, addressed to the District Magistrate. He didn't know what it contained but obviously it was connected to the investigation and if anyone might have known who was responsible for the victim's death, it would have been her own family.

It was raining again when Jim set off soon after they got home from the morning service. Carrying an umbrella and rucksack with a packed lunch that Maggie had made for him, he crossed through Tallital Bazaar and over the Sher ka Danda Ridge, heading for Gyani's village. Before he left the last houses behind, his clothes were soaked. He knew the way and there were several mule trains along the first part of the route, transporting vegetables in from the hills. The muleteers eyed him with suspicion but nobody else seemed to notice the young European setting off on his own.

Half running, he covered five miles in less than an hour, reaching the cobra temple at the top of the ridge where the path descended to Gyani's village. Instead of taking this trail, he cut through the forest directly into the valley along a goat path that kept disappearing in the weeds and nettles. Eventually, he came to an abandoned watermill, where the stream was overflowing because of the rain. The crude slate-roofed structure looked wetter inside than out, though he took shelter for a while, eating a portion of his lunch and lighting a soggy cigarette to calm his nerves before heading on down. Sitting atop the heavy millstone, which no longer turned with the current because the wooden gears were broken, he wondered what he would find.

Fortunately, it began to clear almost as soon as he stepped outside again. By the time he scrambled across the steep hillside and back down to the stream, the sun was coming out. Jim could see a blackened patch of sand at the water's edge, amongst polished white rocks. It looked like an old campfire. The rain had washed most of the ashes away so there were only a few charred pieces of wood and dead coals. Careful not to disturb what was left of the pyre, Jim studied it from different angles. He could see splinters of bone and the cupped shard from a skull that looked like a piece of broken pottery. There was also a half-burned scrap of gunny sacking that Jim guessed had been used to carry the bones. Retreating to a nearby rock, he tried to imagine old Murch dragging the body down here and stacking dead wood on top of the sack of bones before setting them alight.

The streambed was a gloomy place surrounded by overhanging

trees, with only a narrow patch of sky overhead, part of which was bright blue, the rest curtained by monsoon clouds. Jim thought again about the article in *The Pioneer* and asked himself what the truth could be. He wondered if he should keep this secret to himself. By the end of the monsoon the ashes and faggots would have all been washed away, along with the bits of bone. Nobody would ever know what had happened to Cindy's remains, unless, of course, Murch finally confessed. Sitting on the rock, he felt a mournful loneliness come over him, as if the place were haunted.

For a quarter of an hour, Jim remained completely still. He could hear only the murmur of the stream and the dripping of wet leaves. Then gradually he was aware of another sound, so soft it was almost inaudible, a faint rustling in the foliage to his left. Moments later, he heard a click like a pair of dice rattling together. The hairs on his arms stood up straight and he felt his ribs contract. Jim couldn't help but imagine a spirit approaching and he half-expected to see Cindy Bertram's figure, dressed in white, stepping out of the trees. The rustling came closer and he heard the clicking again, a little louder now but still so faint it could have been nothing more than a pebble rolling over in the stream. Last year, when they had hunted here, Gyani told him that the watermill had been abandoned because of an evil spirit that lived beneath the millstone and set it spinning in a counter-clockwise direction, moving against the force of the stream.

He turned his head slowly, facing up the valley. Several seconds later, Jim saw a movement in the shadows. He finally recognized the clicking, as a small, stooped figure stepped out onto the sand. Its four delicate hooves made no sound but the white fangs on either side of the animal's mouth snapped against the rest of its teeth. The musk deer hadn't seen Jim, though it was alert to danger and timidly took several steps forward before lowering its head to drink. The long mule-like ears and soft grey fur made it appear less like a deer and more like an oversized hare. The two incisors protruding from its upper lips were used for digging tubers in the forest, though they looked like a comical attempt at ferocity. Jim knew there was no gentler animal in the jungles of Kumaon than the musk deer. He watched it drink at the stream and then slip back into the shadowy leaves, without ever knowing he'd been watching. If there was a ghost in the valley, Jim thought, it must be himself.

Rising from the boulder, he still hadn't made up his mind if he would tell the police or not. But then he noticed something on the rock. The polished surface had been scratched with another stone. Whoever had sat here before him must have passed the time, while the pyre burned down, by scraping the symbol of a cross on the rock. It was about six inches wide and ten inches long, unmistakable, though crooked because of the rough surface of the boulder.

That evening, when he presented himself at the police station, Jim explained that he had been exploring the valley on his own, searching for mushrooms and fiddleheads, of which there were plenty this time of year. He had carried back a bagful as proof. Though Jim told the police where the pyre could be found, he kept his promise to Gyani and never mentioned his name. Inspector Pearson studied Jim with a sceptical eye, but agreed to send a party the next morning to investigate. He told Jim to be ready by 7 a.m. sharp, to lead the way.

THIRTEEN

'How can you be sure it was her bones that were cremated?' Maggie asked, marking her place in *Agnes Grey* before setting the book aside.

'It's obvious,' said Jim. 'Only a Christian would have scratched a cross on the rock. Murch must have done it.'

'Why would he have burned her?'

'I don't know,' said Jim. 'He had to get rid of the bones somehow.'

'But if he went to all the trouble of digging them up, it makes no sense...'

They were sitting together on the veranda of Gurney House watching the mist swirl across the lake below them, like a painting that kept being erased and then reappearing again within a frame of branches at the edge of the yard. Jim had returned with the police party an hour ago. Pearson himself had gone with them and it took twice as long to walk back because the inspector kept stopping to rest. As soon as he got home, Jim had warmed a bucket of water and taken a bath before changing into dry clothes. His feet were bare and his legs were scratched with thorns.

'They brought back whatever is left,' Jim said, 'a handful of fragments. Pearson says they can be reburied, once the investigation is complete. At least that way there will be something in her grave.'

'I wonder if it makes any difference,' said Maggie.

'What?' he asked.

'Whether you get burned or buried,' she said. 'Either way, you're not coming back from the dead.'

'Doesn't the Bible say we'll all rise up from our graves on Judgement Day?' Jim said. 'That's why they dress you up and put you in a coffin.'

'I don't believe that,' Maggie said.

'Neither do I,' said Jim. 'I think we just go back into the earth, dust to dust, ashes to ashes...'

'Do you ever think you might be reborn in another life?' Maggie asked. 'I mean, like the Hindus believe in reincarnation.'

'Why not?' said Jim. 'It makes as much sense as going to heaven or hell, doesn't it? Frankly, I'd rather come back here to Nainital. It's as good a place as any.'

Maggie glanced over her shoulder at the dark windows of the house. 'We better be careful,' she said. 'Mother will hear us.'

'If you were reincarnated,' Jim said, lowering his voice and looking at Maggie with mischief on his face, 'what would you choose to come back as?'

'A bird, I think. I'd love to fly,' she said.

'What kind of bird?' he said.

'Do I have to choose? Why not just any bird?'

'Well, you might turn into a woodpecker,' he said. 'And it wouldn't be much fun, knocking your head against trees all day.'

She laughed. 'Maybe a hawk or a kestrel. I'd love to be able to hover in the air and soar on the breeze.'

'But you'd have to eat lizards and snakes.'

Maggie made a face. 'What about you?'

Jim thought for a moment. 'A leopard,' he said.

'Not a tiger?' she said.

'No.' He shook his head. 'I'd rather be a leopard. They're much more cunning and hunt only at night.'

'A man-eater?' she said, teasing.

'I'd rather eat venison,' Jim said.

They fell silent for a while, hearing the cicadas starting up in the trees, a rasping sound like a wind-up toy.

'Are you afraid of dying?' Maggie asked.

'Of course,' said Jim. 'But I don't think about it all the time.'

'I'm not afraid,' said Maggie. 'Not even a little bit.'

'Really?'

'Well, I'm scared of the pain and suffering, of course. I wouldn't want to drown or be stabbed to death. But the fact that life ends doesn't bother me at all. It's like reading a book. You come to the last page and you close the covers, and that's it. Finis!' She pointed to the novel that lay beside her on the arm of her chair.

Jim pressed his fingers together thoughtfully and looked out at the sodden pink dahlias growing in the flower beds.

'I don't like the idea of not knowing what happens next,' he said. 'It's not that I don't believe in God, just the uncertainty of it all. I mean, do you think it really matters if we commit sins in this life…if we murder someone? Does that really mean we're condemned to hell?'

'There have to be some consequences, don't you think?' said Maggie.

'I suppose,' said Jim. 'But if a leopard kills someone it's a predatory instinct not a sin. There's nothing cruel or immoral about it, just a matter of survival.'

'Isn't that what makes us different from other creatures?' said Maggie. 'We have a sense of right and wrong.'

Jim shrugged though he didn't look convinced. After a long pause, he said, 'I want to show you something.'

'What?' said Maggie.

'In the godown,' Jim said, getting to his feet. 'Come along.'

She shook her head impatiently. 'I hope it's not some pickled toad or a bandicoot's skull,' Maggie said, lifting herself out of the chair. 'If that's what it is, I'm not interested.'

Jim walked barefoot across the lawn and unlatched the storeroom. It was dark inside and smelled of coal and mildew. He found the candle stub he'd left there last time and lit it. Maggie paused in the doorway. She watched as Jim reached up and took down a matchbox. Shaking the contents into his palm, he held it up for her to see.

'I found this at the cemetery,' he said, 'near Cindy Bertram's grave.'

Maggie stepped into the room and stood close beside him within the flickering circle of light. The tooth looked like a seed, a dry yellow kernel of corn. Shuddering, she wrapped her arms around herself.

'I haven't shown this to anyone else,' said Jim. 'You're the only other person who knows.'

'Why did you keep it?' she said, glancing around at the specimen bottles and jars on the shelves, the horns and antlers, feathers and eggs.

'I'm not sure,' said Jim. 'Somehow, I felt I needed to protect it…preserve it somehow.'

'For what?' she said.

'In case this is all that's left.'

Later that evening, after dinner had been eaten and Maggie and her sisters were washing dishes in the kitchen, there was a knock on the door. Two men carrying a lantern were on the veranda. One of them was Inspector Pearson. Jim stood beside his mother as she opened the door.

'I'm sorry, ma'am, for coming so late,' said Pearson, his face sober though Jim could smell whisky on his breath.

'Please come in,' Mrs Corbett replied. 'What's wrong, Inspector?'

Pearson stepped indoors. He glanced at Jim and nodded.

'Your son has been most helpful,' he said. 'This afternoon, when I showed Mr Murchison the evidence we had gathered, he finally admitted that he was responsible for unearthing Cynthia Bertram's grave. He asked me to give him a pen and paper, so he could write out his confession. We gave him what he asked for, including a glass of water, then left him alone. An hour later, when I went to check on him, he'd filled three sheets of paper with a shaking hand, the words so tightly knotted they're hard to decipher. Then, after signing his confession, he broke the glass tumbler and cut his wrists. By the time we found him and unlocked the door, he was already dead.'

Jim heard his mother suck in her breath.

'I'm sorry, ma'am, for disturbing you at this hour. It's been a sordid business all the way around and I can't say it's ended satisfactorily. In fact, the whole thing's more than a bit of mess.' Pearson looked helpless, defensive.

'Please have a seat,' Mary Jane Corbett said.

'No thank you, ma'am,' the policeman replied. 'I apologize for delivering disturbing news in the middle of the night but I didn't want you hear this from anyone else…what with rumours and all. Of course, there will be more details coming out. But now, if you'll excuse us, ma'am, we'll be on our way.'

Inspector Pearson's eyes circled the room, then rested on Jim.

'Thank you,' he said, putting out a hand. 'Thank you, Jim. You'll make a fine policeman one day, if that's what you'd like to become.'

The upright piano at Gurney House was made in Stuttgart, a handsomely crafted Schiedmayer with a pair of ornate brass candleholders on either side of the folding music rack. It was the most elegant piece of furniture in the Corbetts' home. Often, in the evenings after dinner, the children gathered round the Schiedmayer and Mary would begin to play. Moving chairs aside and rolling up the carpets, they danced polkas and quadrilles. Other times, Maggie would take her seat on the velvet piano stool and play their favourites from Gilbert and Sullivan. As darkness closed in around the house and the long white candles on the piano burned down, the family would sing together, songs from operettas like *H. M. S. Pinafore*. Each of them took turns with the solos but Mary always sang the difficult soprano parts like Josephine's ballad.

> *Sorry her lot who loves too well,*
> *Heavy the heart that hopes but vainly,*
> *Sad are the sighs that own the spell,*
> *Uttered by eyes that speak too plainly;*
> *Heavy the sorrow that bows the head*
> *When love is alive and hope is dead!*

If Tom was around, he might be persuaded to give his rendition of Dick Deadeye, which Jim, though he was a tenor, often tried to imitate, dropping his voice an octave or two, so it sounded more like a grumble than a song.

> *Kind Captain, I've important information,*
> *Sing hey, the kind commander that you are,*

About a certain intimate relation,
Sing hey, the merry maiden and the tar.

After all of the depressing news of the past week, they felt they needed cheering up and even their mother joined in the singing, though Mary Jane Corbett always said she had a deaf ear for music. Three days had passed since poor Murch's suicide. He was now buried in an unsanctified plot of wasteland outside the walls of the cantonment cemetery. Only a handful of people attended the cursory funeral, more out of morbid curiosity than grief. A gloomy pall seemed to have been cast over the town after the case ended so abruptly and without conclusive resolution.

The contents of Murch's confession were sealed until the magistrate had an opportunity to review the case, but in the collective judgement of most residents in Nainital, it was obvious that a pathetic, tormented man had taken his life in an extreme moment of self-loathing, unable to bear whatever terrible things he had done. They assumed that ten years ago, Murch had destroyed a young woman's life and now her memory had been violated as well. Nobody in Nainital felt any satisfaction or sense of justice having been done. But in the weeks that followed, more of the story came out and opinions began to change. Jim had always felt there was something else beneath the surface, which nobody was willing to explain, though everyone seemed aware of the contradictions.

About two weeks after Murch's death, another report appeared in *The Pioneer*. This was written by a correspondent in London, rather than the hyperbolic Mr Kipling. It was reported that a man named Edgar Tunbridge had been arrested while attempting to flee from England to Southern Zambezia. He had been taken into custody by Scotland Yard on charges of murdering Cynthia Bertram in Nainital, in April 1878. The news report went on to state that Tunbridge had visited India a decade ago and frequently passed himself off as a viscount who claimed to be a nephew of the Queen. The case against him would never have come to light if it weren't for recent revelations contained in the written confession of his accomplice, Neville Terrance Murchison, along with substantiating accusations made by the mother of the victim herself.

Suddenly, the lid came off in Nainital.

Virtually everyone remembered Edgar Tunbridge. He had arrived in the summer of 1877, with a letter of introduction from Governor General Lord Lytton, requesting the Commissioner of Kumaon to offer any help and hospitality that might be required. Later, the letter turned out to be a forgery but by then he was long gone. Tunbridge had taken a suite of rooms near the Raymond Hotel and played lawn tennis with Murch and others throughout the summer season. Of all the bachelors in Nainital, he was the most eligible and enigmatic, a handsome young man with a world-weary smile and impeccable manners. In those days there weren't many visitors to the hills who could claim a peerage and the townspeople were in awe of his casual arrogance and well-tailored clothes, the way he danced so effortlessly and invited the younger set to elaborate picnics in the surrounding hills.

'I should have known he was an impostor,' said Tom.

'Why didn't you suspect him?' Jim asked.

'He didn't look like a criminal at all, too well bred, educated at Harrow and Oxford. I took him hunting once or twice, though he was a terrible shot and didn't enjoy walking uphill. More of a ladies' man than a shikari.'

'But why would he have murdered Cindy Bertram?'

'She was going to marry him,' said Tom, without answering Jim's question. 'I remember seeing them sailing on the lake together, just the two of them. Cindy broke off another engagement because of him.'

They were sitting on the veranda and Tom had lit his pipe this time, which had a sweeter fragrance than the cigarettes he usually smoked, though he had difficulty keeping it alight in the monsoon and had to keep striking a match now and then. The girls were still singing indoors and the piano had a cheerful sound, drowning out the dismal patter of rain on the roof. Somehow the news of Tunbridge's arrest had lifted their mood, though nobody knew why or what it meant.

Later, more facts came out, mostly in *The Pioneer*, which reported that Tunbridge had been engaged to Cynthia Bertram and gave her a diamond and ruby ring, which she was still wearing when she died. The ring was said to be worth more than half the houses in Nainital, with stones so perfectly cut they sparkled like stars set in a delicate band of gold. According to Cindy's mother, Tunbridge went away at the end of the season, promising to return before Christmas. That was the last they saw of him and he stopped writing after several weeks. Privately, the family tried to track him down but without success. Eventually, not wanting to create a scandal, they let matters rest. Cindy wasn't the first girl to be jilted, nor would she be the last, though she seemed to believe that Tunbridge would return and continued to wear his ring even after her friends advised her to take it off.

In the spring of 1878, as European families began to return to Nainital, Mrs Bertram brought Cindy and her other children back up to the hills. Three weeks later the girl disappeared. A leopard had been seen in town, lurking along the shore of the lake. When her mutilated body was discovered down the khud, the immediate assumption was that she had been killed by a man-eater. The town readily accepted this explanation, perhaps because it was easier to acknowledge than whatever else might have been the truth. Murch's confession explained what really happened.

He had borrowed money from Tunbridge. Over the winter months, Murch had gone to Calcutta where Tunbridge was living under a different name. They enjoyed a week of drinking together and at the end of it Tunbridge asked Murchison if he could discreetly help him contact Cynthia Bertram. She was carrying his child and he wanted to meet her in private, without her family knowing he was around. Murchison arranged for him to stay in a room he was renting in Haldwani, then spoke with Cindy, explaining that Edgar wanted to see her. According to Murch, all he did was deliver messages back and forth, then arranged for them to meet one night. The next thing he knew Tunbridge was gone and Cindy was dead. Afraid that he would be implicated in the murder, he kept the facts to himself and when the story of the leopard came out, he did not refute it. He believed that Tunbridge, or whatever his real name was, killed his fiancé and their unborn child in order to 'cover his tracks and free himself from any obligations and responsibilities that might pursue him in the future'.

From that day onwards, Murch's life had been unbearable and he began to drink more and more, becoming a hollow wreck of a man. For nearly ten years he didn't hear from Tunbridge, until several months ago a letter arrived from his old acquaintance asking for help once again. The postmaster was kind enough to have it delivered, though Murch had no fixed address. By this time Tunbridge was living in London, having gone through several false identities. Murchison was destitute and desperate. Tunbridge instructed him to dig up Cindy's grave and retrieve the engagement ring which she had been wearing on the day of her death. He calculated the stones alone were worth a thousand pounds and told Murchison that he would give him half that amount if he recovered the ring.

In the darkness of his own despair and degradation, Murchison realized that once again he was being misused, but the promise of sudden wealth and the limitless quantities of opium it would buy left him helpless to his cravings. All he wanted was to shut out the pain. Originally, Murch had planned to rebury the bones as soon as he found what he was looking for. But in the confusion of the night and his own urgent, distracted state, he was unable to locate the ring, so he put all of Cindy's bones in a gunny sack and carried them off, deciding to sort through the remains in daylight. Despite his 'utter revulsion and remorse', he opened the bag the next morning but the ring wasn't there. Now, he was driven by fear more than guilt and addiction, imagining that Tunbridge would accuse him of stealing it for himself. In a panic, he gathered up the bones and carried them into the valley, beyond Sher ka Danda Ridge and burned whatever was left. After that, he tried to escape from Nainital but was arrested at the railway station in Kathgodam, where he was begging on the platform to buy a train ticket.

As for the ring itself, Mrs Bertram admitted that she had removed it from her daughter's lifeless finger on the day they brought her home. For a while she had kept it but the ring was a painful reminder of the heartless cruelty of a man whose nobility was a sham and whose professions of love were nothing but empty lies. In the end, she sold the ring to a jeweller in Bareilly and donated the money to the church.

FIFTEEN

Jim had read The Last of the Mohicans *twice before, yet once again he found* himself absorbed in the forested wilderness of a new world untamed by man. One of his favourite passages described a meeting between Natty Bumppo, better known as Hawk Eye, and Chingachgook, the Mohican brave. They were seated together in the woods. 'Still that breathing silence, which marks the drowsy sultriness of an American landscape in July, pervaded the secluded spot, interrupted only by the low voices of the men, the occasional and lazy tap of a woodpecker, the discordant cry of some gaudy jay, or a swelling on the ear, from the dull roar of a distant waterfall.'

James Fenimore Cooper's sentences, flowing with the syntax of a mountain stream, went on to describe the two men:

While one of these loiterers showed the red skin and wild accoutrements of a native of the woods, the other exhibited, through the mask of his rude and nearly savage equipments, the brighter, though sun-burned and long-faced complexion of one who might claim descent from a European parentage. The former was seated on the end of a mossy log, in a posture that permitted him to heighten the effect of his earnest language, by the calm but expressive gestures of an Indian engaged in debate. His body, which was nearly naked, presented a terrific emblem of death, drawn in intermingled colours of white and black. His closely-shaved head, on which no other hair than the well-known and chivalrous scalping tuft was preserved, was without ornament of any kind, with the exception of a solitary eagle's plume, that crossed his crown, and depended over the left shoulder. A tomahawk and scalping knife, of English manufacture, were in his girdle; while a short military rifle, of that sort with which the policy of the whites armed their savage allies, lay carelessly across his bare and sinewy knee. The expanded chest, full-formed limbs, and grave countenance of this warrior, would denote that he had reached the vigour of his days, though no symptoms of decay appeared to have yet weakened his manhood.

The kinship between the two men, blood brothers, seemed to Jim so natural despite their difference in race. They were allies not adversaries, brought together by a shared humanity and the embracing sanctuary of the forest both knew so well.

The frame of the white man, judging by such parts as were not concealed by his clothes, was like that of one who had known hardships and exertion from his earliest youth. His person, though muscular, was rather attenuated than full; but every nerve and muscle appeared strung and indurated by unremitted exposure and toil. He wore a hunting shirt of forest-green, fringed with faded yellow, and a summer cap of skins which had been shorn of their fur. He also bore a knife in a girdle of wampum, like that which confined the scanty garments of the Indian, but no tomahawk. His moccasins were ornamented after the gay fashion of the natives, while the only part of his under dress which appeared below the hunting-frock was a pair of buckskin leggings, that laced at the sides, and which were gartered above the knees, with the sinews of a deer. A pouch and horn completed his personal accoutrements, though a rifle of great length, which the theory of the more ingenious whites had taught them was the most dangerous of all firearms, leaned against a neighbouring sapling. The eye of the hunter, or scout, whichever he might be, was small, quick, keen, and restless, roving while he spoke, on every side of him, as if in quest of game, or distrusting the sudden approach of some lurking enemy. Notwithstanding the symptoms of habitual suspicion, his countenance was not only without guile, but at the moment at which he is introduced, it was charged with an expression of sturdy honesty...

Maggie was calling. Jim reluctantly put the book down on the side table, swinging his legs off the bed and slipping his feet into the stiff leather shoes he had kicked off half an hour ago. It was time to go to the cemetery. Jim shrugged on his coat, which was too short in the sleeves. His mother complained that he was growing so quickly now that he needed a new set of clothes every six months. Ordinarily, he wore shorts but for the service his woollen trousers had been pressed, though they rose a couple inches above his ankles, even with the cuffs let out.

The women were dressed in formal mourning dresses and even Maggie wore a black hat, handed down from one of her sisters. She looked more feminine than usual with all her lace and frills, the long, slender gloves that reached to her elbows and the Japanese parasol Jim had given her for her fifteenth birthday. He eyed her up and down, then winked, as if to say he approved of his sister's disguise. She straightened his collar and adjusted the knot on his tie. For once, it wasn't raining and it looked as if the monsoon was finally coming to an end. Jim had noticed that some of the ferns were beginning to turn brown and there was a chill in the air that meant the clear days of September and October were almost here. This was his favourite time of year in Nainital, when the forests were still green from the recent rains but the skies remained bright and he could climb Cheena Peak and look across to the high Himalayas arrayed to the north.

Mary Jane Corbett rode in a dandie, carried by four hill men who led the way. The rest of the family followed in a disorderly procession until they reached the churchyard and cemetery gate, where a crowd had gathered. It was a relief to be outdoors in the sunlight after two months of steady downpours and mist. The lake was shining like a polished mirror and the roofs of the town glinted in the afternoon sunlight. Families greeted each other, exchanged handshakes, kissed cheeks and made gentle conversation as they waited for the pastor to arrive. Reverend Olten was still too sick to preside but another minister, Reverend Silverton, had agreed to conduct the graveside service for the reburial of Cindy Bertram's remains. These had been placed in a fresh pinewood coffin. As it was almost empty, the pall-bearers had no difficulty negotiating the steps from one terrace to the next.

Jim recalled how he had climbed over the wall, more than two weeks ago, and felt the haunting loneliness of the cemetery in the mist. Now it was filled with familiar figures, most of them in dark suits and dresses. His own clothes felt uncomfortable and he thought of Hawk Eye's buckskin leggings and moccasins, his green hunting shirt, wishing he could wear the same outfit and put an eagle's feather in his cap. The Corbetts stopped at their father's grave and each of them placed a flower on the stone. Jim left a single white dahlia, taken from the bouquet that Maggie had picked in the garden at Gurney House.

There were so many people in the cemetery, it looked as if most of Nainital had turned up, all of them Europeans, except for the gravediggers who stood to one side, waiting to shovel earth back into the pit. Cindy Bertram's headstone had been cleaned and lay to one side, ready to be replaced. An abundance of flowers had been brought to brighten the grave and dispel the horrors everyone wanted to forget.

They sang hymns and bowed their heads in prayer. Jim thought how much clearer their voices sounded out of doors, without the sombre echoes of church walls. He hardly listened to the pastor's words, reassuring the congregation of God's protective hand. Some of the women, including his mother, wept during the service but mostly emotions were suppressed and subdued. A red-billed blue magpie was calling nearby and Jim caught sight of it flying off in the direction of Sukha Tal. A couple of langurs watched them from the trees below the church.

After the coffin was lowered into the ground, each person tossed a handful of earth into the hole. Jim waited until most of the others had gone ahead before he stepped forward. Maggie caught his eye as he reached into the pocket of his coat and took out Cindy Bertram's tooth. Nobody else noticed as he held it in his palm and scooped up some of the red soil, mixed it together, then dropped it into the grave, as if he were planting a rare and precious seed.

II

THE MAN-EATER OF MAYAGHAT
1926

The killer stalks at night, when hearth fires have burned down to ash and embers, when the air is as still as the earth. Owls and nightjars have fallen silent. Bats return to their roosts. Even the insects, gorged with blood, settle into the torpor of darkness. Only the lisping river continues without pause, a black vein pulsing in the night. The killer makes her way through the forest without being seen, though her eyes penetrate the shadows and her ears are alert to the slightest sound. In the jungle, death assumes many shapes and guises but with the stealth of her approach, the whisper of her breathing and the soft tread of her paws, she is almost formless...like a terrifying dream, or the memory of a violent struggle...intangible fears distilled out of darkness.

Coming down the slope of a ridge between the straight columns of sal trees, she slips into a ravine and crosses a jumble of rocks, avoiding the heavy tendrils of bauhinia vines, hanging like snares that could hold a bull elephant. A bamboo thicket blocks her way as she turns downstream, pausing to sniff at the soft sand, where a spring leaks into a shallow pool. She laps the water gently, as if licking one of her cubs years ago when she was a young mother. Now she is old and thirsty but lured by the same instincts, though her pace has slowed—a festering wound in her right shoulder causing her to drag her forepaw. Yet even with her broken canines and the relentless pain in her leg, she is capable of killing to keep herself alive.

Where the ravine empties into a dry riverbed, and the stream disappears beneath rocks and sand, she cuts across the open ground with a deliberate swiftness, intent on finding the sheltering jungle beyond. The scent of a sambar teases her instincts and for a moment she hesitates, distracted by the deer. But the killer is in pursuit of easier prey.

Ahead, the forest opens into a wide clearing where hundreds of trees have been felled and the sour-sweet odour of sawdust taints the air. Without breaking stride, she passes through a labyrinth of logs and ragged stumps. On ahead, she can just make out the low profile of a canvas shelter. She wrinkles her nostrils at the rank stench of human sweat. The killer has learned to overcome her revulsion for this odour and the fear acquired when

71

one of her cubs was killed and a bullet seared the muscles of her shoulder and left her crippled. Yet this has become the smell of survival now, the only scent that can appease her hunger.

Crouching near a stack of timber, she waits and listens to the murmur of snoring under the lean-to shelter. Traces of wood smoke unspool from the smouldering fire. Exhausted labourers sleep together in a disorderly line, most of them wrapped up against the winter chill. Dew hasn't fallen yet but moisture is gathering in the night air, as the temperature drops and the warmth of the day disperses, allowing condensation to form a humid layer above the fallen trees. If she kills now, there will be plenty of time to feed before first light exposes the layered ridgelines to the east.

Moving forward, she picks her victim—a young woman who lies a few feet away from the others on a pallet of rags, her newborn child beside her. The killer has no sentiments for maternity, though she has borne six litters in her prime. With a sudden rush of controlled aggression, she springs and catches her prey by the throat. The child's mother is dead before she can awaken, teeth puncturing her throat and constricting her windpipe, as vertebrae snap at the base of her skull. The lassitude of sleep gives way to limp gestures of death. The predator hoists her victim in a fluid pirouette, throwing the woman's body over her left shoulder so that her injured forelimb bears less of the weight. Wheeling about in silence, she carries her victim away.

Only the sleeping infant is awakened, wailing for its mother, now gone forever.

ONE

Jim had built the machan using an old string cot that he had tied across the forked branches of a jamun tree, twenty feet above the ground. It overlooked a game trail that crossed the Baur Canal about a mile from his home in Kaladhungi, a place he had known since childhood when he first hunted here with a catapult and muzzle-loader. Jim had spent the night in the tree so that he would be in position at dawn, ready for any animals that passed below his hide. Leaving his rifle at home he had armed himself with a new Rolleiflex camera, purchased a few months back at Hazlett's Studio in Nainital.

The stars were still out when the first birds began to sing and he could see Venus through the branches overhead, a gleaming white pearl above the horizon of foliage. With the crowing of red junglefowl and the syncopated cries of barbets, the sky began to brighten in the east. No matter how many times he witnessed this moment, it always aroused in him a profound sense of elation, as if the world were being recreated before his eyes.

Six years ago, he had returned from his first trip to Europe, commanding the 7th Kumaoni Labour Corps, serving in the war against the Kaiser. Like the five hundred men he led, Jim had never been outside India before. Each morning, camped on those foreign fields, he arose before dawn and listened for the familiar sounds of the jungle but all he could hear were wrens or robins singing in a tattered hedge. For most of their tour, he and his men remained safely behind the front lines, repairing roads and digging ditches. The guns were usually silent at this hour, unless some general had ordered a dawn assault. Mingled with the ambivalence of warfare, he had felt a strange sense of homesickness, a longing that he shared with his men, all of whom were recruited from the hills near Nainital. Jim's greatest satisfaction had been to bring 499 of the 500 Kumaonis safely home. Only one man had died, during the passage at sea. They had done their duty by the king-emperor and returned unscathed. Now, as Jim sat in the machan and waited for light to enter the forest, he remembered another kind of darkness on the fields of France, where destruction greeted the dawn rather than creation, the chemical stench of annihilation. Sometimes, Jim still had nightmares because of what he'd witnessed and he woke with a feeling that everything around him had been obliterated.

But soon the outlines of the trees appeared, their shapes etched against the brightening sky. Two boar shouldered free of the underbrush and trotted below him but there wasn't enough light to take a picture. Then he heard the belling of a sambar, a hundred yards to his right, warning that a predator was on the move. Jim knew each of the tigers in this forest and guessed it might be a young male he'd first seen as a cub two years ago, tumbling after his mother. By now he would be full grown, aloof and restless. The sambar called again, a little closer now. The sound was like a muted trumpet, a metallic cry of alarm. A flock of seven sisters picked up the warning and passed it on by jungle telegraph to a hawk cuckoo that screeched hysterically. Two chital stags, their horns in velvet, came down the path. Jim caught them in the viewfinder, able to make out their spotted coats in the shadows though it was still too dark for a photograph. Their alarm cries, moments later, were higher pitched than the sambar, like the startled yelp of a child.

Jim had positioned himself on his knees, the ropes of the cot digging into his shins as he leaned forward, facing the game trail where it emerged from the jungle. Most animals that passed this way would pause before crossing the narrow Baur Canal, which was three feet wide.

As minutes went by and the forest fell silent, he wondered if the tiger had taken another route, cutting across the canal further up perhaps. It was cold and the camera felt like a brick of ice in his hands. He consciously stopped himself from shivering inside his sweater, a frayed relic from military service, one of the few things he'd brought back from Europe, along with a Parisian vanity set for Maggie, which had a mirror with a painted scene of a boy on the back, playing a lute under a willow tree. She'd laughed when he presented it to her. 'For my boudoir!' she joked, though he could see the delight in her eyes. For his mother, Jim had bought a crystal vase, war loot sold discreetly in a French village. These gifts made it seem as if he'd simply gone as a tourist and returned with souvenirs. Jim hadn't told Maggie most of what he saw of the war. But he'd carried back the empty casings of two brass artillery shells retrieved from a gunner's battery, suggesting they could use them as umbrella stands at Gurney House.

Once more the sambar belled. This time it was less than twenty yards away. Seconds later, he saw the deer step out of the bushes directly in front of his machan, a large doe with a distinctive raw patch on her chest, a sore spot, indicating she was in oestrus. The sambar stamped the ground anxiously, knowing the tiger was close by but unsure of which direction to escape. There was just enough light for a photograph but Jim resisted the temptation, knowing the tiger was likely to follow. He focused on the sambar, her eyes wide with fear as he observed her in the viewfinder.

Then, in a flash, the deer was gone, bolting across the canal and into the trees. Jim's teeth began to chatter from the cold but he clenched his jaw and waited. Ten seconds passed. Twelve. As he counted thirteen, the tiger stepped into view. It was the young male, as he had supposed, a handsome creature with a unique pattern of stripes along both sides of his face that made him look as if he had sideburns. Jim recognized him as he adjusted the focus and pressed the shutter release.

The click of the camera made a sound no louder than the scrape of a match but the tiger heard it immediately and glanced up. His face showed no fear but every feature was attentive, full of concentration. Jim wound the film forward, certain the sound would scare the tiger off before he could take another photograph. Yet the amber eyes continued staring at him, as if the animal recognized who it was watching from the tree above.

After the second photograph, the tiger took a step backwards so that only his head was visible but he allowed half a dozen pictures, before finally retreating into the shadows of the leaves. Altogether, Jim and the tiger stared into each other's eyes for a good three minutes, though it seemed as if an hour had passed. Once he was gone, Jim gave a whoop of delight as he wound the frame forward and closed the camera with excitement. He reached inside his sweater and drew out a cigarette case. Lighting one with satisfaction, he lowered his camera bag to the ground and scrambled down from the tree.

There was no sign of the tiger. As he walked home, Jim calculated the exposure he'd used and went over the shutter speeds in his mind, reassuring himself that the photographs would surely turn out. Ten minutes later, he reached the Kaladhungi Road and walked the last hundred yards to his gate, which had recently been repaired after a herd of wild elephants had knocked it down. As Jim entered the compound, a scruffy mix of stray and spaniel raced towards him, barking eagerly. Stopping to pet Robin, he lit another cigarette and drew a cloud of tobacco fumes into his lungs after a night of deprivation. The first few smokes of the day were always the best, driving out whatever demons were lodged in his lungs.

Maggie was in the kitchen stirring porridge.

'A telegram arrived last night, after you left,' she said. 'A runner brought it down from Nainital. From the Commissioner.'

Jim wiped his camera down with a soft rag and then carefully put it away in its case. Only then did he open the folded piece of paper on which the message had been glued. It was brief and to the point:

MAYAGHAT MAN-EATER CLAIMS FIFTH VICTIM
STOP YOUR PRESENCE REQUIRED STOP
PROCEED IMMEDIATELY STOP REGARDS WYNDHAM

The Indian Railways had an insatiable appetite for wood. Over the past fifty years, the forests of the bhabar and terai, at the foot of the Himalayas, had produced millions of tonnes of billets to fuel locomotives. These chunks of wood powered the boilers, pistons and running gears that hauled goods and passengers across the northern plains of Hindustan. As routes expanded and new tracks were laid, reaching farther and farther into the interior of the subcontinent, millions more trees had to be felled, providing hardwood sleepers or ties onto which the fishplates were bolted, securing thousands of miles of steel rails.

Shorea robusta, commonly known as sal, was the perfect tree to provide a solid foundation of railroad sleepers. There is a saying in Hindustani: So sal khada, so sal pada. Sal trees stand for a century and their wood can lie on the ground for another hundred years. Impervious to termites and resistant to rot even when submerged in water, sal is strong enough to bear the weight of a steam engine and its carriages without warping or cracking. The trees grow straight and tall, so the timber is easily squared off and sawn into sleepers where they fall.

As virgin jungles bordering the Himalayas were gradually depleted of sal, British authorities opened up new tracts of forest for felling. Along the watershed of the Sarda River huge stands of giant sal trees filled the valleys bordering the kingdom of Nepal. The forest department was ordered to supervise extraction of this timber, which was floated down the Sarda and collected at the railhead of Tanakpur.

Five years earlier, following the Great War, the Maharaja of Nepal had donated a million cubic feet of sal from his forests to the British Government in India as a gesture of gratitude and goodwill to celebrate the defeat of Germany. To transport this timber, J. W. Collier constructed a tramline through the Sarda Gorge, a feat of engineering that required blasting a narrow passage across the cliffs below Purnagiri and securing cables to carry the logs down to Tanakpur. Once the timber from Nepal had been transported, most of the tramline was dismantled and subsequent monsoons washed away what little remained. Sal wood is heavy and does not float as easily as pine or cedar but instead of rebuilding the tramline the forest department had determined that if they waited until the river rose with the monsoon floods, there would be enough force in the water to carry most of the timber downstream.

Jim had visited the Sarda Valley on several occasions, most recently a year ago with Percy Wyndham, a close friend and Commissioner of Kumaon. They had spent a week on the river, shooting and fishing. It was one of the most beautiful, unspoiled regions in the Lower Himalayas and Wyndham had debated the wisdom of sanctioning these forests for felling. The timber resources were invaluable but few places were as wild and unsettled as this. They had stayed at Mayaghat rest house, which lay upriver from the gorge, an idyllic site with easy access to the fast flowing waters of the Sarda, where enormous mahseer, as big as seventy pounds, lurked in the pools.

In the evenings, in front of a campfire, they had debated whether these forests should be cut or preserved. The decision rested on Wyndham's signature. Jim had argued that it was one of the few valleys in Kumaon that remained uninhabited and should be protected as a sanctuary for generations to come. He knew that the Commissioner agreed with him but these were critical issues of empire and priority had been given to the railways by the men who ruled India.

Jim had made his career in the railways and he understood their importance, having worked as a freight agent at Mokameh Ghat, overseeing the trans-shipment of goods across the Ganga. The Indian Railways hauled vast stores of wheat and cotton, jute and rice, merchandise of all descriptions from textiles to sugar. It was the lifeline of the country upon which the colonial economy flourished. Who were they to measure the beauty and solitude of a forest against the yardsticks of wealth and commerce? Enjoying a week's sport in the Lower Himalayas might be an unforgettable experience for two English shikaris who had the entire valley to themselves, but how could that be given equal value to the future prosperity of India and Great Britain.

Reluctantly, Wyndham had put his pen to the order and sanctioned the destruction of an unspoiled Eden, bowing to the broader interests of the empire. At the end of the day, both he and Corbett were practical men who understood that painful sacrifices must be made for the greater good. And yet they had both been troubled to think that something as precious and ancient as those jungles along the Sarda would be lost forever.

Now, as he prepared to depart for Mayaghat again, composing a telegram in reply to Wyndham's request, Jim felt a sense of regret that he would see the destruction first-hand. But he was also buoyed by excitement and anticipation at being able to visit the Sarda Valley forests one last time before they disappeared forever.

⁎

He took no more than an hour to pack his tents and other equipment. Jim had everything he required in Kaladhungi neatly sorted and stored from the last time he had gone hunting for a man-eater, six months ago. He spoke to Megh Chand and Khem Chand from the neighbouring village of Chhoti Haldwani. The two brothers often accompanied Jim on shikar, leaving their farms and families in the care of an older brother. A telegram was also sent to Mangal Singh, who lived further back in the hills near Mornaula. He had sailed to France with Jim and was the best camp cook in Kumaon, a master at serving up a meal on short order, though he complained that the sahib hardly touched his food. These men had hunted six other tigers with Jim and knew the risks of going into a jungle where a man-eater was at large but they never hesitated and proudly told stories of the predators Jim had killed. 'Carpet Sahib', as he was called, had already achieved legendary status in the hills of Kumaon for having destroyed some of the most rapacious man-eaters in the region.

A number of practical issues demanded Jim's attention before he could depart. It was the end of the month and his tenants in Chhoti Haldwani had to be dealt with, rents received and salaries paid. From the moment the telegram arrived, Maggie understood that he would be leaving, even before Jim opened the message from Wyndham and read it aloud. She accepted the fact that her brother would never refuse to go after a man-eater, no matter how inconvenient it might be. And Maggie knew better than to ask how long he'd be gone. It could be a week, or a month. Sometimes longer. Jim had plenty of other responsibilities, for the family owned and managed more than a dozen properties in Nainital. Before her death two years ago, in 1924, Mary Jane Corbett had placed most of the business in Jim's hands. The spring season was only a month away and repairs had to be made and houses readied for renters. Locks required changing and rain gutters had to be replaced after heavy snow this year. Jim was also a member of the City Board in Nainital and the first meeting of the year was scheduled in another week. He wrote a note to the Chairman, sending his regrets and explaining that he had been called away to hunt a man-eating tiger on the Commissioner's orders. His reputation as a shikari was well known and the town fathers would not begrudge his absence.

Robin recognized the signs that his master was leaving and sulked on the veranda, whimpering as trunks were carried out and bundles weighed. He often followed Jim into the forest near Kaladhungi and had a keen nose for partridges and peacocks, which he retrieved whenever Jim shot a bird for the pot. But Robin would be left behind. When it came to hunting man-eaters, Jim liked to shed as many responsibilities as he could, as if the hunt were an ascetic pursuit. Compared to the domestic routines and paperwork of being a landlord, hunting had a simplicity that appealed to him, a precise focus and meditative clarity. His men sometimes spoke of it as the 'Sahib's sanyas'. He would retreat into silence for days on end, spending hours alone in the forest, tramping along dirt paths or sitting over waterholes. The only things that sustained him while hunting were tea and tobacco, which he called his two vices. In preparation for the expedition, Jim packed three of his pipes and several pounds of tobacco as well as six tins of Passing Show cigarettes.

Within forty-eight hours of receiving Wyndham's instructions, he was ready to set off. Megh Chand and his brother would accompany the baggage in a bullock cart to Haldwani where Mangal Singh would meet them, while Jim went ahead on foot, a double march alone, so that he could purchase rations in the bazaar. Mayaghat was more than a week's trek from Haldwani but Jim hoped to reach there in six days. He would need porters for the last two stages beyond Tanakpur and sent word in advance. One of the timber contractors he had worked with when he was in the railways, Fateh Khan, would find men willing to carry loads through the jungle. Jim also sent instructions that three young buffalo calves should be purchased and delivered to Mayaghat, so that he wouldn't waste time procuring bait.

The afternoon before he left, he exposed the last few frames of the reel in his camera, taking Maggie's portrait on the veranda, with Robin seated at her side. Then the film was carefully rewound and given to his sister with instructions, asking her to send it up to Hazlett's Studio the next time someone went to Nainital. He also wrote an accompanying note, requesting a set of 4x6 prints. Jim regretted that he wouldn't have a chance to see the results of his wildlife photography until he returned, curious whether the shots of the tiger had turned out.

At four the next morning, two hours before dawn, he climbed out of his bed and lit a kerosene lamp. By its flickering light, he dressed and packed a small rucksack containing his camera and a few personal items as well as money, mostly rupee and anna coins. Paper notes were useless in the hills, away from towns. Maggie got up and made him a cup of tea, which he drank in silence on the veranda. Then, slinging a rifle over his shoulder, giving his sister a kiss on the cheek and whispering goodbye, he departed in the dark while Robin whined at the door. Jim carried no torch and Maggie saw him disappear into the darkness. A minute later, there was the sound of the compound gate opening and closing. It was a cold morning and she pulled her dressing gown about her shoulders and clasped her arms across her chest, shivering from a brief pang of loneliness, as much as from the chill before dawn.

THREE

After five days of forced marches covering a distance of more than a hundred miles, Jim and his men arrived in the Sarda Valley. He had first explored this region while hunting the Champawat man-eater in 1907, a tiger that killed 436 victims. Since then, he had visited the valley several times, most recently a year ago with Wyndham. It was one of the most picturesque areas of Kumaon, especially in March when the flame of the forest trees burst into bloom.

On the forest track to Mayaghat, Jim met the Divisional Forest Officer, Andrew Kincaid, near Purnagiri. The DFO was on his way to Tanakpur to inspect the lumberyards where the timber would be collected after floating down the river. Having been informed of Jim's expected arrival, he greeted him with a guarded sense of relief.

'I hope you'll finish off the damned tiger quickly, Captain Corbett, so these beggars get back to work,' Kincaid said. 'The bastards will use any excuse to slack off.'

Jim offered him a cigarette, then lit one himself. He recognized the Scotsman as one of those crude and arrogant forest officers who hated his job. Red-faced, with eyebrows that flared above a suspicious gaze, he seemed at odds with the forest around him, a man who sought to tame the jungle rather than appreciate its beauty.

'I'll have to see what the situation is,' Jim said. 'When was the last kill?'

'Over a week ago. Since then it's been quiet but the coolies are afraid to move out of their camps. Huddled together like filthy pigs in a sty. I've held back their pay and cut their rations in half but still they won't work.'

'How many camps are there?' Jim asked.

'Three, each of them four miles apart along the river. At least a thousand coolies altogether, mostly from Hazaribagh in Bihar. The blighters never saw a mountain before they got here last summer.'

'And the contractors?'

'Useless buggers. Can't get them to put a fire under the coolies' arses, if I tried,' said Kincaid. 'And to make things worse, there's one of Mr Gandhi's troublemakers stirring up shite.'

Their paths had crossed at a point where the forest track widened and overlooked the river. The Sarda had receded this time of year, flowing much lower than Jim remembered, but still roaring as it crashed and tumbled between sheer walls of rock. Kincaid had a rifle slung across his shoulder and two forest guards accompanied him, both armed with 12-bore shotguns.

'I'll be back in a week,' he said. 'By that time, I hope you've exterminated the tiger.'

'I wouldn't count on it,' said Jim. 'It always takes time.'

Kincaid remounted his horse and set off downriver with his escort.

For the rest of the day Jim and his party met no one else, until they reached the first timber camp. A circular patch of trees had been cut on a narrow plateau above the river. At one end was a makeshift stockade constructed from branches and saplings. Within this enclosure were eight or ten canvas shelters, open on three sides, with fires burning in their midst. The ground was mostly mud, and more than three hundred labourers were crowded together beneath the shelters. From the stench and squalor of the place, Jim could tell that none of them had left the stockade for the past six days. They were too afraid to go down to the river and their only source of drinking water was a muddy trickle that flowed past the camp. The filth and foul odour was overpowering. Jim had never seen anything so desolate and miserable except on the battlefields in France, where trees had stood like skeletons mired within a sea of mud and ordure. A forest ranger, whom Kincaid had left in charge, saluted when Corbett arrived. The inmates eyed the hunter's arrival with sullen expressions, prisoners of their own fear and desperation.

Jim told his men to take the porters on ahead and find a site to pitch their tents upriver from the timber camp, knowing the squalor would spawn disease. The ranger explained that the kill a week ago had happened here. Since then, the labourers had constructed barricades of branches and refused to leave their shelters. A night ago, the tiger had circled the camp, roaring for almost an hour after sunset, but they had shouted and stoked the bonfires to chase it off. He warned Jim about camping nearby, saying the man-eater was sure to attack, for it would be hungry, having eaten nothing for a week.

By the time Corbett caught up with his men, they had chosen a suitable spot on a level spit of land that overlooked the river, half a mile from the timber camp. His forty-pound tent was already pitched and the men were making quick work setting up their tent as well, along with a lean-to that would serve as Mangal Singh's kitchen. Several rocks were rolled together into a hearth. Within half an hour tea had been brewed. Jim took his cup and sat on a rock facing the Sarda, which flowed past in a pleated stream, a perfect stretch of water to fish for mahseer.

Within a few minutes, Jim's reverie was interrupted by the sound of voices accompanied by the clamour of drumming. A party of men arrived carrying empty tin canisters on which they were beating with sticks to ward off the tiger. When they saw the tents, they came running towards Jim and surrounded him in an anxious scrum, all speaking at once.

It took several minutes to decipher what they had to say, but it was clear the tiger had claimed another victim from the second camp upriver. A young boy had been killed around midday, dragged away in full view of his family and others who were too terrified to chase off the tiger.

'The devil showed no fear at all,' the men said. 'It didn't make a sound as it carried the boy into the forest within a minute, no more.'

They explained to Corbett how they had heard that he was coming to hunt the tiger and despite their terror, they had agreed to bring him the news. All of them pleaded with Jim to save them from the marauder.

Two hours of daylight remained. Though Jim had already walked twenty miles that day, he agreed to accompany the men back to their camp. Leaving Mangal Singh with a loaded shotgun and telling him to keep the fire burning all night, Jim shouldered his rifle and put five shells in his pocket, along with his cigarette case and some matches. Then he set off with the party of labourers, who were relieved to have an armed hunter to protect them, though they continued beating on the canisters. The din they created chased off whatever animals might have been around.

Any other day, it would have been a pleasant stroll. The path was level and threaded its way through a colonnade of sal trees, all of which would soon be felled. At several places, there was a clear view of the hills across the river, which lay in Nepal. By now the sun had disappeared behind the ridges and shadows were stretching across the water. Jim stopped only once, to watch a pair of otters tussling on the riverbank, somersaulting over the sand. By the time they reached the second timber camp it was already twilight and fires were blazing.

The dead boy's mother was wailing, along with the other women. This mournful sound added to the pitiful atmosphere. The second camp was similar to the first, though somewhat larger, with two separate enclosures divided by a stream. Instead of a stockade, the labourers had piled up thorns and brambles, which hardly seemed to offer any protection. The same filth and desperation prevailed. With Kincaid having cut their rations they had been reduced to a single meal a day.

Jim asked which direction the tiger had carried off its victim. The party of men who accompanied him were bold enough to take him to the spot where the boy had been killed but from there they would go no further.

Relieved to be on his own at last Jim quickly located pugmarks in the mud and found splashes of blood. His first impression of the prints told him that the man-eater was probably a female because of the narrower shape of the pads and toes, though in the fading light he couldn't be sure. It was easy enough to follow the spoor but once he entered the trees it was almost too dark to track the tiger. Jim assumed the man-eater must have carried its kill into a side valley, west of the camp, where two ridges converged. Moving slowly, he listened for sounds to guide him but there was an ominous silence to the forest, as if all the birds and animals had fled. With his rifle ready and the safety catch released, he made his way alone through the forest, every nerve attuned to danger.

FOUR

Within half an hour of tracking the man-eater, Jim found that the light had diminished to a point where he could no longer see the pugmarks and bloodstains. He was unfamiliar with this area, though he had mapped it out in his mind as best he could, knowing the river lay behind him and the hills rose up to the west. He guessed the tiger was probably feeding on its kill and was unlikely to prowl tonight in search of other prey. Nevertheless, Jim realized that he needed to find a secure place to spend the night. Nothing would have enticed him to retrace his steps and share the crowded, unsanitary conditions of the lumber camp. And by now it was much too late for him to make his way back to his tent. The only alternative was to spend the night in a tree. The question was, which one and where?

The sal trees were impossible to climb, with straight trunks rising forty feet overhead before branching out into a dense umbrella of leaves. Ahead of him, he could see where the ground rose gradually and then pitched up into a thickly forested hillside. Hoping to find a suitable perch for the night, Jim headed towards this slope. Tomorrow morning he would pick up the blood trail again and locate what remained of the victim.

He had no torch or lantern. Because of the man-eater's presence, Jim moved slowly but deliberately forward, with his rifle ready. As the incline increased, he had to reach up and grab at shrubs and vines to pull himself up but soon enough he gained the high ground. Here the forest was a mixed growth of semal, dhak and haldu, which he identified by the silhouettes of their leaves against the darkening sky. He also recognized feathery foliage overhead, with tiny, composite leaves—an amla tree. It grew on the crest of the ridge and seemed about forty feet high, a good, sturdy tree with branches starting eight feet off the ground and opening out into generous spokes. Unloading his rifle, he took a length of twine from his pocket and tied it to the trigger guard, then shinnied up until he could grab the lowest branch, bracing one knee against the trunk. As soon as he was safely aloft, he pulled the rifle after him and worked his way further into the tree. Jim was fifty-one years old, no longer a boy, and climbing trees was harder to do at this age, but he still had the agility and sense of balance that he required. The amla branched in many directions and he found a relatively comfortable seat in the crotch between the trunk and two limbs that bifurcated into a Y, which gave him some stability.

Just as important, there was fruit within reach, for he had eaten nothing since breakfast and the last water he'd drunk was from a spring, soon after meeting Kincaid that morning. Amla fruit is the size of a plum, with a taut green skin and juicy flesh that is intensely sour but with a sweet aftertaste. It is a favourite delicacy of deer, who stand beneath a tree while monkeys raid the branches above. Both sambar and chital gorge themselves on the fallen fruit. Jim recalled, as a young boy, shooting his first chital stag whose stomach was bloated with amla. Having settled himself, the rifle across his lap, he ate a dozen of the sour fruit, which quenched his thirst as much as they eased his hunger.

Knowing there was little chance the tiger would be nearby, Jim took out a cigarette and smoked it slowly. He was tired from all the walking and disheartened by the conditions in which he'd found the labourers living. But after resting in the embrace of the tree, thirty feet above the ground, he felt his spirits begin to lift and the ache in his legs subsided.

Through the filigree of leaves above him, he could see the stars coming out. But the clearest view lay to his left between a gap in the branches where he could trace the black outline of a hill, shaped like a kneeling elephant. From the forest floor below, Jim hadn't been able to spot this hill but now it stood out in the dark, a large mound fringed with trees. He guessed the river circled its base as it flowed down from higher mountains to the north.

While anyone else would have been terrified to spend a night by themselves in an unknown jungle where a man-eater was lurking, Jim felt a familiar sense of contentment. He was happiest when he was alone. Though he would have gladly dropped off to sleep on his camp cot after the exertions of the day, at this moment he felt no drowsiness at all. Instead, he was entirely alert as he let the forest recount its stories.

A jungle owlet was calling close by, its hooting cry like the slow ticking of a clock. The chuckle of a nightjar farther off to his right was intermittent. He could hear crickets and cicadas hidden somewhere in the bark of trees behind him, like someone humming through a Jew's harp. After a while, a chital called near the river but only once and he guessed it must have spooked itself, for there were no further cries of alarm. Jim could read the silences too, those moments in which every sound ceased and the breezes of the day were stilled, so that the amla leaves hung as limp tassels about him. The silence told him that the tigress had lain down after feeding and would guard her kill until the next morning. Later on, he heard a scrabbling noise in the underbrush below his tree but he could tell it was only a small mammal, a civet perhaps or a jungle cat, hunting for rodents.

In another hour, he expected the moon would rise but for the moment all light had disappeared except for the distant flicker of stars above the hump of the elephant hill. Then, to his surprise, he noticed a faint glimmer below the horizon. It was no brighter than a distant star but appeared to be moving through the trees, blinking on and off. For a while, he thought he might be imagining things but the light slowly traced a path up the eastern ridge of the hill. It flickered like a candle flame or a taper of pine. After a few minutes it was gone and the moon finally made its appearance, rising through the branches like a Chinese lantern, a cold, white eye that cast its milky aura over the valley.

At several points during the night, Jim could hear drumming from the nearest lumber camp and the frantic shouts of men, but they were far away and seemed only echoes of the fear and mourning that reminded him of his mission.

He thought of the tiger he had photographed just over a week ago from his machan near the Baur Canal, its eyes watching him with a combination of alarm and complacence. The animal's features had filled the viewfinder of his camera with a mysterious expression, capable of killing him with the vice-like grip of its jaws, yet also strangely reassuring in a way no human visage could be. Their eyes had met through the camera's lens and seemed to suggest a primal kinship, two predators confronting one another in the verdant stillness of the jungle.

FIVE

For a few hours during the night, Jim was able to sleep fitfully, nodding off
a couple of minutes at a time. The seat he'd chosen, in the crotch
of the amla branch, was as stable as a chair and with his back to
the bole of the tree he was able to brace his feet on a lower limb
so that he was relatively comfortable. At points during the night,
he found himself suddenly awake and alert to sounds that might
signal the man-eater's approach but the tigress kept her distance and
eventually the first light of dawn began to filter through the branches.

When it was bright enough for him to see the dead leaves on
the ground, Jim made his way down, lowering the rifle first and
jumping the last eight feet. He then retraced his steps to the point
where he'd abandoned the blood trail last night and began the slow
process of tracking the tigress. If he was lucky, she might still be
on her kill. Jim kept his rifle ready as he patiently followed drops
of blood on the forest floor, as well as the pugmarks, which were
indistinct, except where the man-eater had stepped in a patch of
sandy soil.

It took an hour and a half for him to cover three quarters of
a mile and by the time he found the boy's remains, the sun had
already breached the hills of Nepal and filled the forest with bright
beams of yellow light. The tigress had chosen a cleft hollow in
a dry streambed, where she had stopped to feed. Because of her
injuries she had neither carried the kill too far nor tried to hide
it as most tigers do.

Jim saw the boy's foot protruding above a rock, toes pointing
upward. The calloused sole was a paler colour than the rest of his
dark skin. For several minutes, the hunter stood still and listened,

knowing the tigress could be close at hand. The birds were silent. It was now 8 a.m. according to Jim's watch, and the air was noticeably warmer. He felt a drop of sweat roll down his neck behind one ear and trickle inside his shirt. A light breeze was blowing from behind him and he realized that the tigress could easily pick up his scent.

Step by step, he approached the kill until he could see what little was left of the corpse. The foot was attached to a shin bone, which had been ripped off at the knee, the flesh torn away. Both legs and the torso had been completely eaten. Fragments of bones were scattered about. One arm remained intact, as well as the boy's head, which was turned aside, so that Jim could only see the black mop of hair and the line of his jaw, face down amongst the leaves. Though he had seen dozens of human kills before, the first one on every hunt made him wince and turn away. He glanced up the slope to his right, in case the tigress was watching him from above. But he was sure that by now she had gone to find water and a quiet place to sleep. Perhaps in the evening, she would return. Jim looked about for a suitable tree where he could spend another night, but there was nothing nearby that looked promising, mostly sal trees and a few scrubby ber bushes full of thorns.

With little more to discover, Jim turned around and retraced his steps, walking back down the dry watercourse. He had made a mental note of the place and could see the top of the elephant hill to his left. Moving more quickly now, he headed towards the river. Further down, he came to a small stream but it was mostly stagnant pools and he resisted the urge to kneel down and drink. By now, he could hear the river and as he scrambled over a dead tree that blocked his path, he found a spring flowing out from under a moss-covered rock. After making sure the man-eater was nowhere nearby, he leaned his rifle against a fallen branch, then crouched down and scooped water up with his hands. For almost five minutes he drank, before standing up and wiping a sleeve across his mouth.

Turning around, he was surprised to find himself staring into a set of eyes that held him intently with their gaze. Unblinking, the black pupils met his with a look of intense curiosity combined with suspicion.

The woman was barefoot and carried a bamboo basket under one arm. Her long, black hair was plaited in a single braid. Jim guessed she was in her late thirties, maybe older. Though she had a youthful face he could tell she was no longer a girl.

After his initial surprise, Corbett greeted her in Hindustani. She acknowledged him with a nod of her head.

'What are you doing here?' he asked.

'Collecting herbs and roots,' she said, pointing to the basket, which contained an assortment of leaves and tubers.

'Aren't you afraid to be alone in the forest?' he asked. 'There is a tiger that killed a boy yesterday.'

She set the basket down, along with a small trowel with which she had been digging roots.

'You are alone as well,' she said.

'But I have my rifle.'

'You've come to shoot the tiger?' she asked.

'Yes,' said Jim.

The woman wore a plain cotton sari, wrapped about her in a practical fashion, the pallu drawn over one shoulder and tucked in at her waist and the pleats falling just above her ankles, the way village women tied saris when they worked in the fields or gathered water and wood. Jim thought at first she might be one of the labourers from the timber camp but her accent and dialect were from the hills and she didn't seem to share the desperate conditions of their lives.

'Is your village nearby?' Jim asked.

She looked at him and smiled. 'There is no village but I have a hut, and a small farm for vegetables.'

'You live alone?' he asked, puzzled by her forthright manner. Most women in Kumaon were reluctant to look a stranger in the eye and spoke quietly, averting their faces. But she had a boldness about her, as if she wasn't intimidated by the presence of a white man.

'I live on my father's land, what's left of it that the jungle hasn't reclaimed.'

'And your father?'

'He died several years ago.'

'You have no other family?'

She shook her head and stepped past him to drink from the spring, rinsing her hands before cupping her palm and raising the water to her lips. When she stood up, she wiped her face with one end of the sari.

'Are you with the forest department?' she asked.

'No,' he said. 'My home is in Nainital.'

'I've been there,' she said. 'There were a lot of sahibs like you, and memsahibs with long skirts, riding in boats on the lake. It is a beautiful place.'

'Not as beautiful as this,' Jim said. 'I prefer the forest.'

'Have you seen the tiger yet?' she asked.

'No,' said Jim. 'This morning I found what remains of the boy she killed, about a mile from here.'

'She is old and lame, but her senses are still sharp,' said the woman, as if she were speaking of a person rather than an animal.

'You seem to know her,' said Jim.

'This is her home, just as it is mine,' said the woman. 'We have shared this forest for years and I have seen her often but she has never threatened me. Many times, when I am walking through the jungle, I know that the tigress is watching and I can feel her presence but it doesn't frighten me. She has only started killing people in the past six months, since the labourers arrived. At first, she did nothing but when they saw her near the camps, they were afraid. The DFO tried to shoot her and his bullet grazed her shoulder. He also killed one of her cubs who was fully grown, from her last litter. The tigress escaped though she was wounded.'

'It is not safe for you to be alone in the forest,' Jim told the woman, though he admired her courage. 'The tigress won't see any difference between you and the labourers. She is driven by hunger and she will kill whoever she can.'

The woman laughed. 'How would you know these things?'

'I've hunted tigers all my life,' said Jim, 'and I have learned a great deal from them. Most are harmless and go about their business without endangering our lives. But once they become man-eaters then they must be destroyed.'

'The tigress is protected by the goddess,' she said, in a matter-of-fact voice. 'Without the Devi's blessing you cannot succeed in killing her.'

'Then I will have to appease the goddess,' said Jim, humouring her. 'Is her temple nearby?'

'It lies in ruins, near the old ashram at Mayaghat.'

'Which ashram is this?'

'It was abandoned when the doctor died. My father worked for him as a caretaker. That's how we came to live here. But now the forest guards are threatening me, saying this isn't my land and I must leave. The DFO told me that he would burn down my hut, that all this land belongs to the British sarkar and I have no title to my father's fields. But look at what they are doing, destroying the forest, cutting trees that have stood here for hundreds of years. No wonder the goddess is angry. She has sent her tigress to take revenge.'

The words were spoken softly but with an undertone of bitterness.

'Who was this doctor?' Jim asked.

'An old man who retired here to the forest and taught us which herbs to collect and what their uses were and how to dry and preserve them. The doctor was a good man and he treated me like his own daughter but he died a long time ago, when I was still a girl. Everything I know, I learned from him and my father.'

'What are those herbs?' Jim asked, pointing at her basket. 'What will they cure?'

'This one is called motha; the roots are dried and used for dog bite,' she said. 'And this one, kundaru, expels kidney stones. These leaves are from the mehndi plant, which is a cure for baldness.'

'I could use that,' said Jim, taking off his hat and running a hand over the sparse hairs on his scalp.

She laughed and picked up her basket then placed it on her head.

'Goodbye,' she said, turning away.

'Be careful,' said Jim.

Glancing back at him, the woman laughed and walked away into the forest.

SIX

The three-mile trek back to camp took Jim less than an hour. The men were relieved to see him, though they were used to his absences when hunting tigers. Sometimes he disappeared for several days at a stretch. Mangal Singh got breakfast ready while Jim went down to the river to wash up. The Sarda was swift and clear, with white sand and rocks along the shore. The shock of plunging into the cold current took Jim's breath away but he submerged himself three times before wading out onto the bank, refreshed and fully awake. For a moment, he was tempted to fetch his fishing rod and try a few casts but decided he would save that for another day.

As he was drinking his third cup of tea and smoking a pipe after breakfast, Jim explained to his men what had taken place the night before.

'This evening, I'll go back and sit up over the kill,' he told them. 'Then if the tiger doesn't return, we'll move our tents tomorrow. The DFO has said we can have a room in the forest bungalow at Mayaghat. It will be safer there and more centrally situated so I can cover most of the valley, up and downriver.'

'Why not move today?' said Mangal Singh. 'That way, the porters can go back tomorrow. There's no reason for them to stay.'

Megh Chand nodded in agreement.

'It depends when the buffaloes arrive,' said Jim. 'If they are here before noon, then we can shift to the forest rest house. Until then, I'll get some rest.'

After his long vigil in the amla tree, he was grateful to lie down. Within minutes Jim was asleep on his cot. He slept soundly for several hours until a babble of voices woke him. The buffaloes had arrived from a village above Tanakpur and three men accompanied them. The animals were young males, less than a year old, with wild white eyes and hides as black as the night. They were restless and the men had ropes around their necks and bamboo staves to control them. As there was still plenty of time to go ahead to the rest house, they packed up and set off. Jim led the way, carrying his rucksack and rifle.

After a mile, they came to a sizeable stream, where the buffaloes stopped to drink. A short distance away, Jim noticed a tawny fish eagle in a tree overlooking the stream. Suddenly, the bird plunged from its branch. With talons extended it took a small fish from the water and returned to its perch. Quickly unpacking his camera from the rucksack, Jim left his rifle and circled through the bushes along the streambed. Moving as stealthily as possible, he got within thirty feet of the eagle, which was busy eating the fish. The light was good and Jim was able to take a picture but when he tried to go a little closer, the eagle heard him and flew off with the fish in its claws.

By two o'clock that afternoon, they arrived at the Mayaghat rest house. Like most forest bungalows it had a corrugated tin roof covering two large rooms, with a veranda on all sides. A short distance away stood a line of storerooms and quarters, occupied by the caretaker and forest guards. An apron of lawn surrounded the bungalow, which looked out across the river towards a tributary that flowed in from Nepal. It was an idyllic scene, framed by two small jacaranda trees planted five years ago, when Collier's tramline was being built. These were in bloom, the blue flowers adding a bright contrast to the many hues of green.

Last year, when Jim and Percy Wyndham had stayed here, they camped in luxury, for the Commissioner travelled with his retinue. They had uniformed bearers who served their meals on bone china with silverware and wine glasses carried all the way from Nainital. Though he enjoyed the forest as much as Jim did, Wyndham liked to be comfortable and lived in style. During their visit, the Mayaghat rest house had been transformed into the Commissioner's residence with fresh linens and all the accoutrements that accompanied Wyndham when he was on tour. He even had his own personal thunderbox and trunks of official documents, sorted and filed away by his munshis and clerks, who travelled with him wherever he went.

After Jim inspected one of the rest house rooms, which had been emptied for his use, he instructed the men to set up his tent in the yard and told them that they could stay in the bungalow. The other room, which Kincaid occupied, was locked. When Jim explained the arrangements to the forest ranger, he began to protest, saying that the Sahib should stay in the rest house, while they would make room for his men in the quarters.

Jim shook his head. 'There's not enough space for them, even after the porters leave. They'll be more comfortable in the rest house. And I prefer my tent.'

He saw the look of consternation in the ranger's eyes. 'But, Sahib, the man-eater...'

'Most of the time, I'll be sitting up for the tigress at night. Why waste the room?'

'The DFO Sahib...' the ranger began to protest.

'I'll speak to him when he gets back,' Jim interrupted. 'I need my men to get a safe night's sleep.'

He knew, of course, that Kincaid would disapprove of housing Indians in the rest house and the ranger was only trying to follow orders. But Jim assured him that it would be all right.

After he had settled everyone and eaten a quick meal of cold rotis and a little dal that Mangal Singh had saved from the day before, Jim had another cup of tea and a cigarette, then set off through the forest to find the kill. He now had his bearings, for the elephant hill lay directly north of the bungalow. Cutting across at an angle through the forest, Jim located the dry streambed where the body lay. It was four o'clock as he cautiously approached the kill, aware that the tigress would soon return.

The problem of where to sit up remained. None of the nearby trees offered a suitable seat. Jim decided it would be better to position himself under the lee of a large rock, twenty feet above the boy's remains. He didn't relish the thought of sitting on the ground but the rock would protect his back and there was no easy line of approach for the man-eater, except up the streambed. By this time the corpse had begun to decompose and there was a faint smell of rotting flesh, though the breeze was blowing away from him.

He had learned from years of experience that man-eaters played by different rules than the rest of their species. Most tigers avoid human contact and the slightest scent of a hunter makes them turn away. But man-eaters are drawn to the odour of human beings, though they have an uncanny ability to distinguish between those who seek to kill them and others whom they can safely devour. Time and again, Jim had been amazed by a tiger's instinctual ability to avoid a hidden threat. Often, after an unsuccessful night sitting up for a man-eater, he had seen where a trail of pugmarks approached his hide, then turned away from danger at the last minute, as if someone had put up a sign announcing his presence.

As he settled into position, Jim could see the boy's foot and the uneaten portion of the shoulder with the arm attached. Several crows and a pair of magpies had discovered the kill and once Jim was in position, they began squabbling over the remains. He was relieved to see them, for the birds would immediately warn him of the tiger's arrival.

For an hour, the scavengers picked at the flesh. Some time later, they were joined by a jackal that came timidly forward and shared in the feast. There was no sign of the man-eater as darkness fell. During the night a procession of different animals arrived to inspect what was left of the body. The first was a porcupine that sniffed about and then left with a rattle of quills. Somewhere around midnight, after the moon had risen, two civet cats came by and sampled the remains. Jim could smell their foetid odour despite the stench of decaying flesh. A jungle cat and a couple of wild dogs put in an appearance. Even a small sounder of wild boar showed up to avail themselves of the tigress's largesse. None of them realized that a hunter was sitting nearby. Clouds kept covering the moon and then dispersing, so that the forest shifted from pale light to complete darkness. Then, just before daybreak, Jim saw a large shape approaching. It appeared some distance below him, a fluid shadow that seemed to flow amidst the rocks. For a few minutes, Jim wasn't sure if it was really there but then the shape appeared closer, gliding over and around the boulders on the opposite slope, forty yards away.

He lifted his rifle slowly to his shoulder, avoiding any sudden movement but bringing his weapon in line with the creature. It seemed large enough to be the tigress but he couldn't be sure. Waiting, Jim leaned forward and listened, then heard the crack of a bone, a sharp, brittle sound. He could see the white rocks that marked the location of the kill but there was no sign of an animal. His eyes ached from the strain of trying to locate the tigress until the clouds finally parted and in the moonlight he saw the ghostly shape of a large animal feeding on the kill. Jim's finger tightened on the trigger and the rifle's sight was fixed on his target. A second later the gunshot rang out and the recoil pushed Jim back against the rock. Instantly, his finger found the second trigger but by then the animal had rushed away and now there was silence.

SEVEN

The clouds had closed in again and it took another hour for grey light to fill the forest. Jim cradled his pipe in the palm of his hand but did not light it, for he was still seated on the ground and if the tigress was nearby, the odour of tobacco smoke would give away his position. When he finally felt it was bright enough for him to inspect the kill, Jim got up stiffly. The rifle he was using was a double-barrelled Jeffrey's .450/400 Nitro. He had killed several tigers with it already—an accurate weapon with plenty of stopping power for large game. Immediately after firing, Jim had reloaded the right chamber and pocketed the spent brass casing.

As he made his way down the slope, the heels of his shoes dug into the soft earth and he clambered over a loose scree of small stones that funnelled into the streambed. While hunting, Jim preferred to wear light shoes rather than boots, for he could tread more softly and it was easier to climb trees and negotiate thick brush without being weighed down by clumsy footwear.

Each of the scavengers that night had taken their share of the remains and little was left except splinters of bones and a few scraps of flesh. Jim's eyes were focused on finding fresh blood and he knew exactly where his target had been. Though he was prepared for the sudden charge of a wounded man-eater, Jim was also meticulous in searching for clues but he found no sign of the tigress. Instead, as he cast about in a widening circle, he discovered fresh prints of a large male leopard and it became clear what had happened.

Like all the other creatures that night, the leopard had come to feed on the tigress's kill, another opportunistic scavenger who seemed to have no revulsion for human flesh. For a moment, Jim considered the possibility that the man-eater might actually be a leopard but it was unlikely and he dismissed the idea as he followed the tracks for several hundred yards, up and over the crest of the ridge, where the leopard had escaped. There was no trace of blood and the animal seemed uninjured, for it had bolted without pausing. At one point, he could see where the leopard had torn through a patch of dense creepers and its claws had raked the leaves in its hasty retreat. After an hour of trailing the leopard, Jim concluded that he had missed.

Now, at last, he could smoke his pipe, for the tigress had obviously abandoned her kill and the leopard had got away unscathed. Heading back to camp, Jim puzzled over the fact that his bullet had gone astray at such close range. He put it down to poor light and clouds passing over the moon, casting deceptive shadows. Nevertheless, he was relieved not to have killed the leopard, which was guilty of nothing more than scrounging for a free meal, though a wasted bullet always nagged his conscience. From boyhood, he had learned to economize on ammunition and never carried more than five shells at one time.

Back at the forest rest house, his first priority was to clean the rifle, running a soft brush and then rags through the barrel and wiping it down with an oilcloth, for dew had settled on the steel during the night. Jim squinted through the barrel and saw that the grooved spiral bore of the rifle was clean.

Though he had spent the whole night awake, Jim had a busy morning. He needed to pay off the porters as well as the men who had brought the buffaloes. They all set off together at a hurried pace, for they hoped to reach Purnagiri by nightfall and Tanakpur the next day. Then, with the help of the two brothers, Megh Chand and Khem Chand, Jim tied up one of the buffaloes. They tethered it near the lumber camp at a spot Jim had noticed earlier where a strangler fig had overwhelmed another tree. There was a murky pool of water and plenty of grass nearby. When they left the animal, it was grazing contentedly, unconcerned about being abandoned to its fate. The bell around its neck clanked loudly.

On their way back from tying the bait, Jim and his men came upon the woman he had met the day before. She was gathering berries from a bush near the rest house and watched them go by with an amused expression on her face. When Jim greeted her, she laughed.

'What happened, Sahib? Last night I heard the gunshot,' she said. 'Did you kill the tigress?'

'No,' he said.

'I warned you,' the woman said, with a mocking tone in her voice. 'Your bullets will always miss.'

Megh Chand turned towards her in annoyance. 'Be careful what you say,' he said. 'How dare you speak like that?'

Her smile disappeared but the woman stood her ground.

'I'm only speaking the truth. No hunter can kill this tigress.'

'The Sahib has killed many tigers,' said Khem Chand. 'How would you know whether he will succeed or fail?'

'Let her be,' said Corbett quietly, starting to move on.

Once more the woman laughed and then demanded, 'Does the Sahib have a cigarette for me?'

Khem Chand turned on her. 'Have you no shame!'

But Jim put a hand on his shoulder and restrained him. 'It's all right,' he said.

Taking the silver case from his pocket, he picked out a cigarette and handed it to the woman. Then he lit a match and watched her lean towards the flame that wavered between his cupped hands.

'The tigress has killed six innocent people,' he said softly. 'She is old and injured. I must put an end to her life.'

'Why?' said the woman, drawing on the cigarette. 'So the forest department can continue felling trees?'

'No,' said Jim. 'So the labourers won't live in fear.'

Leaving her, they returned to the rest house, where Mangal Singh had prepared a midday meal. Jim was hungry and ate the rice and dal quickly, burning the roof of his mouth. He was puzzled by the woman but also intrigued by her independence and lack of fear. While everyone else was terrified of the man-eater, she seemed completely unafraid, wandering about in the forest on her own.

'She is an evil woman,' Khem Chand said, as he took away Jim's plate. 'They say she is a witch.'

'Who says this?' Jim asked.

'The forest guards and the caretaker of the bungalow. She knows how to cast spells and summon ghosts. That is why the man-eater does not harm her.'

'I don't believe these things,' said Jim.

'I'm only saying you should be careful, Sahib,' Khem Chand replied. 'She is a dangerous woman.'

That afternoon, Jim asked the ranger to take him to the labour camp, where he met the father of the boy who had been killed. He offered to accompany him to the spot where his son's remains could be collected for cremation. The labourer's eyes were full of grief and terror. For the past week, he had not stepped out of the camp and Jim wondered how long these people could continue to live like this, under hellish conditions, trapped within their own horror and despair.

'Don't worry,' said Jim. 'The tigress has gone away from here and moved upriver. I will go with you and my rifle will protect us.'

The father seemed undecided but two others offered to go with him and soon the small party headed out of the camp and into the forest. At the streambed they collected what little was left of the corpse in a bundle of cotton cloth. None of them spoke and they eyed Jim anxiously as he led them back to the riverbank. While the father and the others built a small pyre on the sand, Jim stood guard. The last rites were performed without ceremony and they used Jim's matches to set the kindling alight. Within a few minutes the blaze flared up and orange flames were reflected in the flowing water, as the smoke drifted downstream with the current. The crackle and roar of the pyre dissipated into the silence of the forest.

As Jim watched the men squatting solemnly to one side, he thought how desperate their lives must be; yet he admired their courage and dignity in this moment of sorrow and wondered at the trust they had placed in him.

EIGHT

A light rain began to fall just before dusk and it grew colder than it had been since their arrival, a thin veil of winter mist settling over the valley. After two nights without sleep, Jim turned in early and drifted off to the soft patter of rain on canvas. He slept deeply and without dreams. The loaded rifle lay on the trunk beside his cot and the tent flaps were securely tied but if the tigress had come that night, she would have had no difficulty claiming another victim. Yet Jim was not afraid, for he felt sure the man-eater had moved farther up the Sarda Valley, towards the third lumber camp. He had often spent nights like this, protected only by the taut fabric of his forty-pound tent. Jim preferred it to the claustrophobic rooms in a forest rest house with the windows and doors bolted shut, full of bed bugs and other insects, spiders and scorpions.

The next morning, he was up at five thirty, just as the first streaks of light appeared over the mountains of Nepal. Last night's rain had cleared the air and Jim watched the last stars burn out and listened to the croaking of giant hornbills across the river. Ten minutes later, he heard the loud beating of wings, as a pair of the large, ungainly birds flew across the river and landed somewhere in the trees below the rest house.

Mangal Singh was stirring and got up to light the fire for tea, while Jim set out to check on the buffalo. It was a fifteen-minute walk and he found the calf lying quietly where they had left it, with a resentful but placid expression on its face. Nothing had disturbed it during the night, so he checked the rope to make sure the knot was still secure and returned to the rest house. Two cups of sweet tea and a couple of cigarettes were all Jim needed before he set off upriver. The ranger had told him that the third camp was four miles away, where a large stand of sal trees was being cut. No victims had been taken from this camp as yet but the labourers had stopped work and were living under the same confined, unsanitary conditions.

Walking alone through a forest in the foothills of the Himalayas at this hour of the morning, with the leaves and grass washed clean by the rain and the sun gilding the upper branches of the sal trees, is an experience that cannot be matched. Jim almost forgot about the man-eater as he made his way through open glades and tunnels of foliage, listening to bulbuls and laughingthrushes. He saw very few animals, other than a couple of wild pigs that broke cover as he passed by and a chital with her fawn. Because of the felling of the forest, he guessed that most of the game had retreated farther into the hills. The steel barrels of his rifle were cold and his breath condensed in clouds but the exertion warmed him, even before the beams of sunlight penetrated the canopy of leaves.

About a mile beyond the rest house, he had to ford a stream and took off his shoes to wade across. Just as he set off again, climbing up the opposite bank, he saw a movement in the grass and a cobra crossed his path. It was about four feet long, the colour of gunmetal. As Jim took a step backwards, the snake turned and spread its hood. Looking about for a stick, Jim snapped off a dead branch the length of his arm. The cobra held its head two feet off the ground, swaying slightly. For a long moment, it seemed as if it was preparing to strike. Jim lunged forwards and swung at it but holding the heavy rifle in his other hand, he could not put his full weight behind the blow and the cobra slid away unharmed, disappearing into the brush. Disappointed, Jim threw the stick aside. He had a superstition that whenever he was hunting a man-eater, he first had to kill a snake before he could succeed in shooting the tiger.

In the soft dirt along his path, he found pugmarks but these appeared to be of another tiger for they were smaller than the ones he'd seen the day before and there was no evidence of injuries. He estimated that the Sarda Valley must be home to four or five tigers and there were probably an equal number on the opposite side of the river. This time of year, when the water was low, a tiger could easily swim across at places where the current was not too swift.

On earlier visits to the Sarda Valley, Jim hadn't come this far upriver. He and Wyndham had hunted and fished downstream from Mayaghat. When they had asked if anyone lived up here they were told that no villages lay within two days' walk of the rest house and the forest was so thick a man would get lost forever in the tangled foliage and maze of ravines.

Eventually, Jim came to another side-stream, which he was able to jump across, stepping from stone to stone. The labour camp was still on ahead but he saw a ruined wall, where the stream met the river. Rising above the wall was a spreading mango tree. Remembering what the woman had told him about an ashram, Jim's curiosity was aroused. Leaving the trail to investigate, he followed the stream and soon came to the stone wall, which was broken at places. Beyond this was a small temple and a low building with creepers growing up one side. At first, it looked deserted but then Jim noticed a laundry line with a towel draped over the rope. He called out a couple of times in Hindustani, until there was the squeak of a door being opened. A man's voice cried out, 'Who is it?'

'A visitor,' Jim replied. 'I mean no harm. May I speak with you?'

The voice came from the other side of the buildings. 'Please wait, I'm coming.'

'There is no hurry,' Jim said. 'Take your time.'

He saw the movement of a figure coming through the overgrown garden and a young man appeared. Seeing Jim, he stopped in his tracks, with a look of surprise and confusion.

'You're an Englishman,' he said, then added, 'From the way you speak Hindi, I wouldn't have guessed.'

Now it was Jim's turn to be taken aback. He hadn't expected to find someone who spoke perfect English, here in the forest. They stared at each other in disbelief.

'I'm Captain James Corbett, from Nainital,' said Jim, extending a hand.

'Bimal Swadeshi,' the other replied, shaking hands. 'You're a hunter?'

Jim nodded. 'I'm here to try and kill the man-eater.'

'Of course,' Bimal answered.

'And what brings you here?' Jim asked.

'I'm a Congress party worker,' said Bimal. 'I was sent here to work with the Banrajis, they're forest dwellers.'

Corbett studied the young man, his hand-spun cotton clothes, the earnest but guarded look in his eyes. He had a light woollen shawl draped over his shoulders. During the past few years, Jim had met a number of Congresswallas and found most of them naive or self-serving, sometimes both.

'Why would you bring your politics here to the jungle?' he asked, without disguising his distrust.

Jim had little time for Mr Gandhi and his preachings, though he agreed with him on many things, such as the abolition of caste and uplifting the poor, but when it came to his statements against the British authorities in India, he found the rhetoric offensive.

Bimal laughed. 'Everything is politics, I suppose,' he said. 'Even your tiger hunting.'

'How's that?' said Jim.

'Please come in, Captain Corbett,' said Bimal. 'I live very simply and I can offer you nothing more than a cup of black tea.'

This gesture of hospitality eased Jim's suspicions, as he followed Bimal through the gate of the ashram and into the complex. The ruined walls enclosed about two acres altogether, though much of it was overgrown and the buildings looked as if they hadn't been lived in for years.

'The Banrajis. I know of them as Ban Rawats. They are a tribal community, am I right?' Jim asked.

'Yes, a few of them live here during the winter months. In summer they move further back into the hills. They are hunters like you,' said Bimal. He pulled a stool out for his guest, placing it on the veranda of the main dwelling. The walls were cracked and stained but it was a solid structure.

'Is this your property?' Jim asked.

'No,' said Bimal, putting twigs in the hearth and starting the fire while they spoke. 'This ashram was built by a man named Atma Ram, an Ayurvedic doctor from Lucknow who renounced material wealth and retreated to the forest, as all good Hindus are supposed to do. At the age of seventy he came here to live and spent the next ten years in quiet contemplation. Upon his death the ashram was abandoned.'

'You live here alone?' Jim asked.

'Yes, for the past year. I've made a few trips out, as far as Tanakpur and Nainital.'

'But where is your home?' Jim asked.

'Allahabad, though my parents are Bengali,' he said. 'And where in England are you from, Captain?'

'Nowhere,' said Jim, taking out his cigarette and offering one to Bimal, who politely refused. 'I was born in Nainital.'

'Ah,' said Bimal. 'Eurasian?'

Jim shook his head. 'My ancestors were Irish but we've been in India for three generations, since 1794.'

'Then you're almost an Indian, like me,' said Bimal with a laugh. Jim guessed he was in his mid-twenties, just out of college.

'Swadeshi, that isn't your real name is it?' he asked.

Bimal shrugged. 'No, I chose it for myself. As you must be aware, Mr Corbett, Hindu names reveal our caste and I believe we should erase all social labels.'

Jim nodded. 'And how do you plan to help the Banrajis?'

'Honestly, I do not know,' Bimal said. 'When Gandhiji was visiting Allahabad, I asked him what I could do and he told me to search for the poorest people I could find. He said, "When you find them, go there and live amongst them. Learn their language and try to understand their situation. Then you will know what must be done."'

'Mr Gandhi is an impractical idealist,' Jim said.

'Perhaps,' said Bimal with a guarded frown. 'I would have preferred to be sitting in protest rallies and shouting slogans against the British, or joining others to fill your jails. But he chose this path for me.'

'Exiled to the jungle,' said Jim. 'I would say you're a lucky man. There aren't many places as peaceful as this.'

He waved his cigarette towards the junction of the side-stream and the Sarda, which lay in front of them across the garden wall, a beautiful stretch of sand and boulders surrounded by unspoiled forests.

'Yes,' said Bimal, adjusting the pan of water on the fire and adding tea leaves. 'But now your forest department is destroying the valley, cutting all the trees.'

'It's for the railways,' said Jim. 'Progress. Mr Gandhi should be thanking us for this. He likes to travel by train, I'm told.'

Bimal laughed again. 'Yes, and the poor labourers have been brought from Bihar to fell the trees. They're virtually slaves, treated like animals. Though I came here to work with the Banrajis, Captain Corbett, I think I've finally found my cause.'

'What's that?'

'These labourers have no voice, no rights. I must speak up for them because what the British are doing is unspeakable.'

Jim was silent for a moment, remembering the squalor and misery of the camps.

'The man-eater has only made things worse,' he said.

'That's true.' Bimal nodded. 'But the forest officers, especially this man Kincaid, are as ruthless as the tiger, as heartless...'

'Tigers are neither ruthless, nor heartless. Those are human traits,' said Jim. 'They kill only for their survival.'

'And why do you kill, Captain Corbett?'

Jim inhaled, then blew out a smoke ring before replying.

'To protect those who are too terrified to step outside the fences they've made for themselves.'

'And once you destroy the tiger, what will happen to them?' Bimal asked. 'Who will protect them from the British?'

'I suppose that's your job, not mine,' said Jim, impatiently.

A tension had grown between them. As Bimal removed the lid from the boiling tea, they both fell silent. Jim watched the young man dig around in a sack near the hearth.

'Unfortunately, I have no sugar,' said Bimal. 'With the tiger's presence, there's no way to get supplies from Tanakpur. But I put black pepper in my tea. It's very healthy, especially in winter.'

'I've never tried it,' said Jim. 'But I suppose there's always a first time.'

He watched as three peppercorns were crushed and added to the boiling tea. Several minutes later, Bimal strained the steaming brew into a pair of brass tumblers and handed one to Jim.

'Have you seen the tiger yet?' Bimal asked.

'No. I sat up for it two nights but without much luck. My guess is that it's moved into this area. I hope you have a sturdy bolt on your door at night.'

'I do,' said Bimal, sipping his tea.

Jim raised the glass to his mouth and sucked the searing liquid between his lips, slurping to help cool it down. The pepper burned his throat but the taste was not unpleasant.

'Do you like it?' Bimal asked.

'Not bad,' said Jim. 'I could get used to it. But doesn't Mr Gandhi disapprove of tea? I've heard he speaks against it.'

Bimal smiled. 'I suppose we all have our weaknesses.'

Just then, there was a noise beyond the garden wall. Both of them heard it, a soft rustling of leaves, as if a large creature were brushing through vines and creepers. Jim set his tea down and reached for the rifle, which was resting against the veranda wall. A minute later, two figures appeared from behind an overgrown hedge. They were both barefoot and dressed in loincloths. One of them had on a tattered army shirt, while the other was barechested and carried a bow and a handful of arrows. The older of the two held a wooden vessel in his hands, sealed with a stopper carved out of the same kind of wood. Seeing Jim, their eyes filled with alarm, as if they had suddenly come face to face with a tiger.

NINE

The Banrajis continued to watch Jim with wary eyes. They had brought honey for Bimal, who made another pan of tea and sweetened it this time. Jim tasted the honey, which had a sharp wild flavour and contained bits of wax and even a few dead bees that had to be picked out. The two men said they had collected it the day before from a hive in the forest.

'Where do you live?' Jim asked them.

They pretended not to understand his question but when Bimal prompted them, they pointed towards the elephant-shaped hill.

'How long does it take you to walk there?' Jim asked.

'Only a short while,' they said, and he realized that hours or minutes meant nothing to them. Their Hindustani was broken and awkward, barely fluent enough to answer simple questions.

The two men accepted the glasses of tea from Bimal and spoke softly between themselves in a language Jim could not understand. The Banrajis looked more Nepali or Tibetan than Indian. The man without a shirt had scars on his right shoulder where something had clawed him.

When Jim asked what creature had attacked him, he said in a matter of fact voice, 'Bear,' with no further explanation or story.

'Has the tigress killed any of your people?' Jim asked.

The two hunters shook their heads, as if they were unaware of the man-eater.

'It's killed six of the labourers so far,' said Bimal. 'Have you seen it?'

'Yes, there are plenty of tigers around,' they answered vaguely.

'She's an old tigress, with a wound in her right foreleg,' Jim said. 'Do you know where she is right now?'

One of the men swallowed his tea, then spoke: 'We saw her prints this morning, heading in that direction.' He pointed farther up the valley.

'Can you show me the prints?'

They seemed not to hear the question but after a minute or more the two men got to their feet and set off. Jim thanked Bimal for his hospitality and followed. Though the hunters barely acknowledged his presence, they let him follow them into the forest, and he could see they were skilled trackers who moved through the jungle with ease and confidence. After half an hour, they came to a low escarpment covered with trees, where a section of the slope had collapsed. The debris from the landslide was mostly clay and, crossing the lower edge, were the pugmarks of the tigress. One of the hunters pointed them out to Jim, who studied the prints, recognizing the elongated pads and toes, as well as the smeared mark where she dragged her right paw. The man-eater had passed here more than twelve hours ago, before the rain fell, for sections of the prints had washed away.

'Where will she go from here?' Jim asked the Banrajis.

'Who knows?' said the one man gesturing upriver. 'Somewhere in that direction.'

Taking out his cigarette case, Jim offered the Banrajis a smoke. They accepted the cigarettes and took the box of matches from him. When the older man passed it back, Jim told him to keep the matches, which he gladly did, tucking them away carefully in a pouch at his waist. For a few minutes they smoked in silence.

'Have you shot a tiger before?' the one man asked at last.

'Several,' said Jim. 'Mostly when they kill human beings.'

'And you've come here alone?'

'I have three men with me. We are camped near the forest bungalow at Mayaghat.'

'Where the other Englishman stays?' Jim could hear the man's voice change and saw a look of concern in his eyes.

'Has he threatened you?'

Both men nodded. 'He fired his gun at us,' said one. 'He tells us we cannot hunt here. We caught a barking deer in a snare and he took it away from us.'

Jim stubbed out his cigarette and exhaled the last of the smoke.

'Are there wild boar in this forest?' he asked.

'Plenty,' said the Banrajis in unison.

'If you show me a boar, I'll shoot it for you,' Jim said.

The hunters eyed him and then glanced at his rifle. Without another word, they got to their feet and set off in the direction of the elephant hill. It wasn't long before they came to a clearing from where Jim could see smoke rising above the trees. He knew this must be the third lumber camp though they circled around it, the Banrajis keeping their distance and staying within the cover of the forest.

Soon afterwards, they climbed up over a steep ridge and then descended into another streambed where the underbrush grew thicker, a mix of thorns and bamboo. Jim could see that the hunters were suddenly more alert, slowing their pace. Twice they stopped to listen. Then, as they passed under the arched branches of a semla grove, the lead hunter froze and pointed. A hundred yards away, Jim could see a movement in the bushes. He slipped the safety off and stepped ahead of the Banrajis. A moment later, three boar raced out of cover and scrambled up a slope. They were moving too fast for Jim to risk a shot but just as they were about to cross over, one of them stopped and looked back. The leaf sight on the rifle was set for closer range but Jim compensated by aiming just above the shoulder. The report of the .450/400 was as loud as the crash of a falling tree and the Banrajis cringed at the sound. But their eyes were fixed on the boar, which toppled over in its tracks, then rolled back down the slope.

TEN

The elephant hill rose directly above the place where Jim had shot the boar.
Cutting a stout branch, the Banrajis tied the dead animal by its feet
with vines and lifted it onto their shoulders. They set off at a quick
pace despite the weight, cutting across to the eastern ridge of the
hill, which ascended from the river. Soon they joined a well-defined
path and after half a mile arrived at a cluster of limestone crags
jutting above the forest. Jim could see a wisp of smoke rising out
of a natural chimney in the rocks. After climbing a stone staircase,
they arrived at the Banraji settlement, a complex of cave dwellings
laid out according to the contours of the ridge. Marking the location
in his mind, Jim realized that the lights he'd seen the first night in
the amla tree must have come from here.

A dozen or more children darted out to greet the hunters. Seeing
the boar they broke into a clamour of excited voices. Only when
they spotted Jim did the children fall silent. From every side, he
could feel the scrutiny of watchful eyes upon him. Several women
emerged from the caves to see what was happening and three other
men scrambled down to help carry the boar into the middle of the
settlement. Amidst the rocks was an open space about forty feet in
diameter, like a level courtyard. Jim unloaded his rifle and rested it
against a rock before sitting down.

His two companions spoke to the others and gradually a babble
of voices resumed. Jim watched the children approach the boar,
running their hands over its stiff black bristles and touching the
bullet hole in its shoulder. Today, there would be enough meat for
everyone and Jim could see the men discussing what to do next.
Above the open space were three caves, each about the same size.

The openings were walled up with stones and fitted with narrow doorways framed in wood. The forest dwellers had made themselves as comfortable as possible under primitive conditions. All the younger children were naked and the adults, both men and women, wore very few clothes though they had a simple modesty about them. Compared to the desperate conditions in the labour camps, it was a clean, hospitable site. Firewood was stacked in piles and the shelter of the rocks gave the community a protected feeling, like a tiny fortress built by nature with craggy battlements and a warren of passages between the stones. On one side of the courtyard lay a fire pit where the men began to stack dry brush and sticks before setting these alight. Once the smoky blaze got going, four of the men lifted the boar onto the fire to burn off its bristles. The children squealed with delight and Jim felt their attention had finally shifted away from him. The smoke smelled of singed hair.

Rising to his feet, Jim explored the settlement. Women moved away shyly as he peered into the caves. These were dark and airless but neatly swept and furnished with wooden stools and woven mats made of split bamboo. Outside one of these caves sat an old man carving a wooden vessel, chipping away with a crude instrument like a miniature adze. One of the man's eyes was blind, a creamy white colour. The other eye observed Jim impassively.

As he ascended to a second level, the view opened out below him and from a promontory of limestone slabs, he could look down upon much of the Sarda Valley, where the river circled the foot of the hill in a crooked S. Farther south, Jim could see the third labour camp and bare sections where trees had been felled. Some distance beyond, he spotted the roof of Bimal's ashram hidden amidst the jungle. Downriver, beyond the ribbed outlines of lateral ridges, he could just make out the Mayaghat rest house and the second timber camp. From their roost in the limestone caves, the Banrajis had a hawk's-eye view of the valley as well as the destruction of the forest.

'What are you looking at, Sahib?' a familiar voice asked. 'Can you see your tiger from here?'

Jim turned and met the woman's eyes. She was standing outside the doorway of a cave, her arms folded across her chest.

'Are these your people?' Jim asked, surprised to find her here.

'No, but I have known them for many years, since I was a girl,' she said. 'One of the women is expecting a child and I've come to help her with the birth.'

Smoke from below carried with it the smell of the roasting boar.

Sniffing the air, the woman said, 'I hear you've shot an animal for them. Has your rifle regained its accuracy?'

Jim took a seat on a flat rock and studied the woman, puzzled by the way she taunted him. From within the cave came a whimpering cry, a girl calling out for help. After glancing inside, the woman smiled and said, 'It will be a while. Her first child.'

Squatting down across from Jim, she gestured for a cigarette. He gave her a disapproving look but took the case from his pocket and offered it to her.

'So, how do you survive out here in the jungle?' Jim asked as he lit her cigarette and then his own.

'I make do as best I can,' she said, evasively. 'These people share with me whatever they gather in the forest—honey, wild fruit,' she said. 'But I earn a living in other ways.'

'How's that?' said Jim.

'Each season there are different roots and plants which I collect and dry. Then twice a year, the vaids and hakims send their agents to buy herbs from me. My father started this business. It is easier work than farming and I earn enough for my needs. This forest is full of herbs that can cure almost every disease,' she said, her voice no longer mocking but sincere and serious.

'This morning I met the young Congress worker who lives at the ashram. He told me that he was trying to help the Banrajis,' said Jim.

'Yes, Bimal. He arrived last spring,' said the woman. 'My hut is close to the ashram and he often comes and eats a meal with me. He talks about things I don't understand but I enjoy his company.'

'How will he help these people?' Jim asked.

'Who knows. He's just a boy who wants to change the world,

but he means well, and I'm glad to have someone to talk with once in a while.'

'You have no husband?' Jim said.

'No,' she said. 'My father tried to marry me off but I knew I would never be happy as a housewife.'

From inside the cave dwelling came another startled cry of pain as the birth pangs grew more intense but the midwife ignored her patient.

'And you?' she asked. 'Are you married?'

'No,' said Jim, shaking his head.

'You live alone?'

'My elder sister lives with me,' he explained. 'We have a family home in Nainital and a farm in the terai.'

'What is your sister's name?' the woman asked.

'Maggie or Margaret.'

'Maggie,' said the woman, pronouncing it softly as she blew a stream of smoke through her lips.

'And your name?' Jim asked.

'Kaiyu,' she said. 'My father called me that. I am named after the goddess these people worship. Kaiyu Devi. She is a forest spirit to whom the Banrajis pray before hunting.'

'So they worship you?' said Jim.

'No, my father liked the sound of the name, that's all,' she replied, laughing.

'My name is Jim,' he said, as if it were the polite thing to say, since she had introduced herself, but their names added an awkward element to the conversation, a personal note that hadn't been there before. The woman placed her cigarette carefully on a ledge beside her and disappeared inside the doorway. After several minutes she came outside again.

'There is still some time,' she said, putting the cigarette to her lips. Then, after a pause, she continued. 'The tigress is on the other side of this hill. She is resting now but tonight she will begin to hunt again. Early this morning she was calling near the river. Right now, the tigress is asleep, though the pain in her leg disturbs her and flies keep settling on the wound. Soon she will get up and drink at the stream that flows from the other side of this ridge. Then she will go to the forest camp and kill one of the labourers if she can.'

'How do you know all this?' Jim asked.

She made a casual gesture with one hand. 'I know these things.'

'Why wouldn't the tigress come here and kill one of these people?'

'She might. But they know how to protect themselves and their forest gods watch over them. It is easier for the tigress to take one of the labourers from the camp.'

Another choked cry came from the cave and Kaiyu flicked the butt of her cigarette aside and stood up. 'I must attend to her,' she said.

Jim got to his feet and descended to the open courtyard below, where the boar was being butchered. Its steaming carcass had been cut open, the offal and entrails removed and lying to one side on a bed of fresh bauhinia leaves. The meat would be divided and each household would cook its share. One man was removing a hind leg, his knife moving expertly as he cut through the joint. Grinning, the hunters invited Jim to stay and share their feast but he said he needed to return to Mayaghat before it grew dark. He loaded the rifle again and the breech snapped shut like a steel trap.

ELEVEN

Kincaid had arrived at the rest house a couple of hours before Jim returned.
When he found Mangal Singh and the others staying in the room
next to his, he threatened to horsewhip them if they didn't clear
out immediately. By the time Jim got there the DFO's temper had
cooled but he was still irate at the indignity of sharing the rest
house with natives.

'Captain Corbett, there are forest department rules and we must
enforce them. Our rest houses are for European officers not fucking
Indians,' he said, his voice trembling as he tried to control his rage.

Jim usually avoided confrontations but he spoke his mind. 'I
don't see what difference it makes,' he said.

'The next thing you know, they'll bloody well be wanting to
share a railway compartment with us, or walk along the Upper
Mall in Nainital,' said Kincaid. 'I kept that room empty for your
use, not theirs.'

'I prefer my tent,' said Jim. 'And under the circumstances, their
safety is my first consideration. If I am to succeed in shooting this
man-eater, I need to make sure that my men are safe and well rested.'

'What do you think the damned quarters are there for?' Kincaid
snapped.

'You've got twelve men staying in two rooms. They can hardly
breathe in there,' Jim replied, without raising his voice. 'But, in any
case, it doesn't matter. We'll be moving camp tomorrow, heading
upriver. The man-eater has shifted to the northern end of the valley.'

Kincaid's small grey eyes examined Corbett with the dull
indifference of someone whose mind can never be changed. Jim
had known men like him all his life. He often wondered why they

stayed in India, if they hated the place and the people so much.

'Has there been another kill?' Kincaid demanded. He was standing at the edge of the rest house veranda, his khaki uniform stained with sweat, a cigar between his lips. Jim stood below him, the rifle cracked open over one arm.

'Not yet but your third camp is completely unguarded and I'm willing to bet the tigress will choose her next victim from there. I would suggest you dispatch two of your forest guards, armed with 12-bores, so there's some protection.'

'I don't have guards to spare,' said Kincaid, 'especially not to do sentry duty for a bunch of half-starved coolies.'

'The reason they're starving is that you've cut their rations. That's a short-sighted decision. They're the only ones that are going to move those logs for you.'

'I'll manage my own business, Captain Corbett,' said Kincaid. 'And I'll thank you to stick to yours. Where do you plan to set up your camp tomorrow?'

'There's an old ashram on the riverbank. It's a relatively safe place for my men.'

'That fucking Gandhiwalla lives there,' said Kincaid. 'He's been stirring up more trouble than the tiger. I've notified the police but, of course, nobody listens. Nobody has time to flush out troublemakers in the forest.'

'Tomorrow I'll need the help of two of your men to carry some of our equipment and supplies,' Jim said.

'I told you I don't have men to spare,' the DFO replied abruptly.

'Mr Kincaid,' Jim spoke in an even voice. 'The Commissioner of Kumaon has sent me here and I'm sure he would be disappointed to learn that the forest department hasn't been cooperating with our efforts to eliminate the man-eater.'

The dull grey eyes responded with a glint of resentment. Kincaid's complexion turned an even brighter shade of red but he conceded. 'What the hell, you can take three of the guards and the forester too. The beggars are terrified to go out on their own.'

'Thank you,' Jim replied and headed for his tent. Another hour remained until sunset and he headed down to the river for a wash. This time, he also took his fly rod. A few casts into a clear, fast-flowing stream always calmed his nerves. He rigged up a flyspoon with a gaudy red tuft of dyed wool and junglefowl feathers. It was a lure of Jim's own design and most mahseer found it irresistible. Megh Chand accompanied him. Within half an hour, Jim landed three good-sized fish, all of them above ten pounds. Taking out his camera he snapped a photograph of Megh Chand holding the mahseer.

Sending the catch up to the rest house, Jim quickly stripped and dove into the river, feeling the cold exhilaration of the water. Swimming against the current for several minutes he let the grime and sweat of the day wash off. Feeling the stubble on his chin, he resolved to shave the next morning, hearing Maggie's voice in his inner ear, admonishing him. She had never liked his moustache—calling it a 'caterpillar' on his upper lip—but the beginnings of a beard were enough for her to banish him from the house forever. After towelling off and changing into a fresh set of clothes, Jim felt revived. Picking up his fly rod, he headed back to his tent.

Kincaid was sitting on the veranda of the rest house, still smoking his cigar. He called out to Jim as he went past.

'No hard feelings, I hope, Captain Corbett,' he shouted. 'Why don't you join me for a drink this evening, before we eat your fish?'

'I'm afraid I don't drink spirits,' said Jim, 'but I'll come and smoke my pipe.'

A *peace pipe*, he thought to himself. He would have rather spent the evening alone but knew that things would be easier if Kincaid was on his side. The men had pitched a second tent near his and he assured them the tiger was unlikely to come around tonight. They seemed unconcerned.

'If you are safe outside,' said Khem Chand, 'so are we.'

Mangal Singh spoke up. 'The foresters are saying there's cholera in the first timber camp. Two people have died but their relatives were too frightened to cremate the dead. A burning coal was put in their mouths and the bodies were thrown in the river.'

'If I don't shoot this tiger, we'll all be dead before long,' Jim said.

'There could be an epidemic. Make sure you boil our drinking water.'

Just after the sun dropped below the ridge to the west, Jim put on a sweater and walked across to the rest house. Kincaid had already poured himself a whisky and the bottle sat beside his chair.

'Are you sure I can't persuade you to have a nip?' he said.

'No, thank you,' said Jim, settling into the chair and stuffing his pipe. Somewhere off in the jungle a barking deer was crying out in alarm. Probably a leopard, he thought, or maybe it was frightened by its own shadow.

'You know, I've heard a lot about you, Captain Corbett,' said Kincaid.

'Nothing that would condemn me to prison, I hope,' Jim replied.

'No. They say you understand the jungle better than any native shikari.' Kincaid eyed his drink before taking a swallow of the amber liquid.

'I learned to hunt alongside poachers when I was a boy,' Jim replied. 'We kept one eye out for forest guards and the other was focused on game.'

Kincaid laughed. 'The forest service is a thankless job,' he said. 'No matter what happens we're always to blame. If some fucking Burra Sahib arrives to go hunting and we can't produce a tiger for him, we're told that we haven't done our job protecting wildlife, but then if a man-eater kills a dozen natives, we're held responsible for their deaths. What are we to do? This is the jungle after all.'

'There was a time when I thought I'd join the forest department,' said Jim. 'It would have been a natural career for me but I chose the railways instead.'

'An equally thankless job,' muttered Kincaid. 'If a train is late, it's your fault. But if some bleeding VIP arrives on the platform after the train's pulled out, they'll shout and swear at you for being on time.'

'Most of my work was handling freight at Mokameh Ghat. Fortunately, bundles of jute and cotton don't complain if they're late,' said Jim. 'But I like to think we got most of our shipments delivered on time.'

His pipe smoke drifted up under the eaves of the rest house

and in the darkening sky, he saw a flock of green pigeons skimming the treetops.

'I'll be honest with you, Captain Corbett,' said Kincaid, pouring more whisky into his glass. 'I'd quit this job in a flash if it meant I could go home.'

'Where's home?' Jim asked.

'Glenrothes, in Fife,' said Kincaid. 'It's not much of a place but a damn sight better than this. And the whisky tastes better too.'

'I'm told that Scotland has beautiful forests, especially the Highlands.'

'Aye, but it's all owned by English gents who come up and shoot grouse every season, then leave the land to rot the rest of the year. We had a farm that my brothers sold after my father died two years back. Then they drank up the money, including my share. Bastards. Now one brother is dead and the other's a tenant on his own property, paying rent to work our father's land. There's justice for you.'

'What will you do when you go back?' Jim asked.

'I don't know,' said Kincaid. 'My pension won't take me very far and my wife's run off with some swine…better he has the bitch than me… Who knows, I'll find a couple of rooms in town, as far away from any forest as I can be. Frankly, Captain Corbett, I'd be happy if I never saw another tree in my life. Cut 'em down, as far as I'm concerned.'

'Well, if you clear the Sarda Valley, that could be your revenge,' said Jim.

Kincaid swore under his breath, then laughed. It was a strange sound, bereft of humour, a throaty groan of drunken anguish that seemed to echo some dark joke he'd recalled from years ago.

'First, you've got to shoot the bloody tiger,' said Kincaid.

'I'll do my best,' said Corbett. They sat on the veranda as the sun went down, looking out across the river. A flight of egrets went by but Kincaid seemed unaware of the beauty of the scene. He spoke instead of his disgust for his superiors, the Conservator who had posted him here to this 'godforsaken hellhole'.

Jim interrupted him. 'By the way, I met some of the Banraji tribals. They might help me locate the man-eater. Nobody knows this forest as well as they do.'

Kincaid shook himself out of his stupor and stared at Jim with those same dull eyes he'd seen this afternoon.

'Vermin,' he said, 'Fucking vermin. They're vile, wicked men, no better than jackals, Captain Corbett. Don't trust those tribals an inch, I tell you. I'd sooner put a bullet through their brains than follow them through the jungle.' Kincaid's anger surfaced again and his face was flushed.

'What harm do they do?' Jim asked. His pipe had gone out and he let it hang from the corner of his mouth, watching Kincaid sidelong.

'Cruel bastards,' the DFO continued. 'Worse than wild dogs. They'll clear out a forest of animals before you know it.'

'I doubt they kill any more than the odd leopard or tiger,' said Jim. 'Mostly birds and small game.'

'Aah! What would you know!' said Kincaid, slumping back in his chair.

'The Banrajis don't have an easy life. Their ancestors were here in these forests, long before any of us arrived,' said Jim. 'I admire their fortitude.'

'Fortitude!' said Kincaid. 'Fucking fortitude. I wouldn't waste fancy words like that on them. They're cunning bastards and poachers. So's that whore who consorts with them, digging up roots to brew her evil potions. As if I didn't have enough trouble with the contractors and coolies...'

Jim got to his feet and excused himself, saying he had to get an early start the next morning. Kincaid was already too drunk to stand on his feet and there was no point in continuing the conversation.

TWELVE

When Jim and his men arrived at the ashram, Bimal Swadeshi gave him the news. The tigress had claimed another victim from the third timber camp at the northern end of the valley, just as Kaiyu had predicted. Bimal agreed to let Jim and his men stay in the ashram complex and he showed them a room near his, which could be swept clean and made secure by stuffing thorns in the open window and barring the door with planks of wood. Leaving Mangal Singh and the others to settle in and tend to the buffaloes, Jim headed off immediately.

When he reached the timber camp, he was aware of the hostility in the labourers' eyes. Most of the men sat sullenly in the shade of a canvas shelter, while the women were huddled to one side. Seeing an Englishman, several of the labourers began to demand their wages and rations. Outnumbered, Jim wondered if he would find himself beaten up by an angry mob, but after he spoke to them and explained that he wasn't a forest official and he'd come here to kill the tiger, they were grudgingly placated.

Jim learned that the previous evening the tigress had killed a young woman who had gone to the edge of the camp to collect sticks from a stack of brushwood. As she and two others were chopping a dry branch, the man-eater appeared. They screamed for help and ran away but the unfortunate woman was caught from behind and dragged into the forest. She was no more than sixteen and her husband was a year older, though he looked like a child, with tragic eyes that stared through Jim, as if unable to comprehend his loss.

The entire camp had witnessed the attack, which occurred just before dusk. Nobody had slept that night. What little firewood there was had been burned up by midnight and none of them dared collect any more, for fear the man-eater might return.

Jim found the tracks of the tigress in the mud near the edge of the jungle along with scattered drops of blood. A little later, he found the woman's sari which had snagged on a barberry bush, six yards of frayed cotton, torn almost in half. By now he could easily recognize the man-eater by her pugmarks, the elongated toes and the way her injured paw left a smudged impression. The surrounding ridges rose steeply out of the valley and directly ahead, more than a mile away, stood the elephant hill where the Banrajis had their cave dwellings. The tigress had made her way up a low ridge but then turned aside before reaching the top. Unable to negotiate the rough terrain, the man-eater had chosen an easier line through some scrub until she descended into a clearing where a large pipal tree stood beside what looked like a natural altar of stones.

As Jim approached the place, he was struck by the symmetry of the clearing and the way the rocks stood in a ring, though they were much too heavy for anyone to have positioned them like this. The massive pipal must have been older than all the other trees by at least a hundred years. Its trunk had a circumference of fifty feet or more with branches that stretched out to encompass the clearing, as if keeping the other trees at arm's length.

The man-eater had crossed between the rock formations and passed directly in front of the tree, where a large pool of blood indicated that she had laid her victim down and rested here before moving on. Jim held his rifle with one finger on the trigger and stepped cautiously around the tree, where he could see drag marks in the leaves. The blood trail continued for another ten yards into a shallow depression surrounded by more rocks, where the body lay uncovered. Jim could see the victim's torso wedged between two boulders. He moved forward cautiously for there were plenty of places where the tigress might be crouched and waiting. But, eventually, he was satisfied that she had abandoned her kill, and he carefully examined the body.

Very little had been eaten, except for a few mouthfuls from her lower back and buttocks. The rest of the girl's body was intact.

Looking down at her, Jim thought she looked like a nude figure in a painting or a sculpture, one of those women carved into the brackets of ancient Hindu temples, a yakshi or forest spirit. Staring at her like this, he felt suddenly embarrassed, as if he were a voyeur. The corpse was completely naked and her hair was open across her shoulders. The girl's face was strangely calm, her mouth set in what might have been a smile, though the open eyes seemed to reflect the terror she'd experienced before the tigress sprang on her. Her throat was bruised and punctured, but there was little blood. One of her hands lay across her bare breast, as if in a gesture of modesty, while the other was flung out, seemingly grasping for help.

Circling round the body, Jim could see where the tigress had gone up a side valley to the right. He knew she was probably lying up for the day and nursing her wound. The fact that so little of the kill had been eaten was an encouraging sign, for the tigress would surely return that evening. Scanning the trees, Jim saw that one of the branches of the pipal stretched out above the kill. Though the main trunk went straight up for almost thirty feet it had plenty of handholds and footholds for him to climb. Jim felt sure that he would be able to find a suitable seat for the night.

Taking a final glance at the body, he wished he could cover the girl's nakedness but knew that the tigress would shy away if the body was disturbed in any manner.

As he retraced his steps to the clearing, Jim noticed once more how the boulders seemed to stand upright in a loose circle, like a ruined amphitheatre consumed by the forest. Yet there was no evidence of a human hand, not a single inscription or figure etched in stone. As Jim stepped around one of the large rocks, he saw a fluid shape slide across his path, a rat snake about three feet long. Instinctively, he picked up a rock and hurled it at the snake, striking it in the middle of its back, so that it stopped immediately, writhing in pain. Taking another stone, Jim smashed its head. The snake kept twitching, as he flipped it over with the toe of his shoe. Though he realized it was irrational and the snake was harmless, Jim felt his anxiety ease, convinced his luck was about to change.

The sound of footsteps startled him and looking up, he saw Kaiyu approaching, making her way down the ridge with a bamboo basket in one hand. Three Banraji hunters accompanied her. One carried a spear, while the other two were armed with light bows and arrows that looked like children's toys, though Jim knew they were deadly weapons in the hands of these practised hunters. The Banrajis hadn't seen Jim and he stood still until they were within fifty feet, when he raised a hand to his mouth and gave the alarm call of a frightened chital. Immediately, the hunters stopped in their tracks, sharp eyes alert. Jim was hidden behind one of the larger boulders. After a minute, he repeated the cry, then followed it up with the hoarse bark of a langur. The hunters turned their faces upward, trying to locate the sound. Seconds later, Jim stepped into view and called again.

He could see Kaiyu smile as the Banrajis looked at each other, confused to find an Englishman in front of them, instead of a deer or a monkey. They approached him with caution, though they recognized who he was from the day before.

'You're lucky they didn't shoot you,' said Kaiyu, with a laugh. 'Their arrows never miss.'

'So, you delivered the child?' said Jim.

'Yes, a boy with an auspicious birthmark on his hand,' she said. 'I was given this basket as a gift.'

Jim gestured with his head, towards the spot where the body lay beyond the pipal tree. 'The man-eater has killed another labourer. Her corpse is over there.'

Kaiyu glanced in the direction he indicated, as if she already knew where it lay. At the same moment, one of the hunters discovered the dead snake. The Banraji said something to his companions, then lifted its limp body with the end of an arrow, holding it up for the others to see.

'You killed it?' Kaiyu asked, concern in her eyes.

Jim nodded.

The Banrajis spoke in agitated voices though Jim couldn't understand their words.

'This is a sacred spot for them,' said Kaiyu. 'This pipal tree and the rocks that surround it. They call it the shrine of Diho, their sun god. On certain days they worship here and it is forbidden to kill anything within sight of this tree.'

'Even a man-eater?' said Jim, as one of the men flung the snake aside.

'Who knows? It's what they believe,' said Kaiyu. She turned to the men and spoke to them in their own language, gesturing with one hand. After a few moments, the Banrajis turned away and headed back into the forest and up the hill.

'What did you say to them?' Jim asked.

'I told them, now that you were here, I didn't need their protection,' she replied. 'I told them the Sahib would walk me home.'

THIRTEEN

Kaiyu's hut was half a mile from the ashram, on the opposite side of the stream that flowed into the Sarda. Abandoned fields skirted the farm and there was a corral of thorns and branches where goats had been kept at one time. Her hut was made of stone and solidly built with small barred windows and a sturdy wooden door. The roof was slate and there were two rooms inside, one where she cooked and slept, the other where she stored her herbs. An assortment of roots and leaves lay drying outside in the sun and a couple of chickens were wandering about. Though she had been away from home for two nights, it looked as if nothing had been disturbed. Jim was surprised that here in the forest no predators had taken the chickens. Behind the house was a small vegetable garden with cucumber vines, a few rows of peas and some beans growing up a makeshift trellis. The river lay a hundred yards away, down a steep embankment edged with bhimal trees, which had been coppiced. A line of stunted figs also grew along the perimeter of the garden.

'Have you eaten today?' Kaiyu asked as they arrived at the hut.

'No, but my men will have prepared my food,' Jim said.

They could see smoke rising above the ashram.

'Then have a cup of tea, at least,' she said.

On their way to the hut, Kaiyu had told him how her father had worked part-time as caretaker for the man who built the ashram, Atma Ram, doing some of the heavier chores, cutting wood and carrying water. At the same time, he cleared the land and built this hut. Growing up here, Kaiyu had known nothing else and it had been a simple, lonely childhood. She also told him that the Banrajis gathered rare herbs and she bartered with them, trading sacks of rice and flour for medicinal roots and seeds.

Jim settled himself on a wooden bench outside the hut, as Kaiyu went inside and lit the fire. Smoke began to trickle out from under the slate slabs on the roof. Still puzzled by her solitary life, Jim wondered how this woman could live alone in the middle of the forest.

'Don't you feel unsafe out here?' he asked, when she emerged from her hut and squatted near the door. 'Nobody threatens you?'

She laughed. 'Do you mean men or animals?'

'Both,' said Jim. 'It's a lonely place.'

'The animals seldom bother me, though sometimes they come and eat my vegetables or carry off a chicken now and then,' she said. 'As for most men, they are afraid of me because they believe I'm a witch.'

Jim passed her a cigarette.

'Are you a witch?' he asked.

'What do you think?' Kaiyu brushed a strand of hair away from her face and her eyes shone with amusement.

'I don't believe in witchcraft,' Jim said.

Kaiyu studied him with a serious expression, then waved the smoke away with one hand and got up to go inside again. Two minutes later, she emerged and handed him a brass tumbler of tea. It was made without milk but sweetened with honey.

'Right now, the tigress is lying beneath an overhanging rock, sheltered from the sun.' Kaiyu spoke in a distracted voice, as if picking up a story she had left unfinished. 'She is in pain. From time to time, she licks her wound...'

Jim interrupted her. 'If you know where she is, why don't you tell me? I'll go and shoot her.'

'It would do no good,' said Kaiyu. 'She will hear you coming and slip away, or maybe she will ambush you. The tigress knows that she is being hunted. She knows that an Englishman with a rifle is stalking her through the forest. This Sahib is a brave man and understands the secrets of the forest. Now that he is here, she must be more careful than before.'

Stubbing out his cigarette, Jim took a sip of tea.

'Being a witch, you know all this?' he asked.

Kaiyu laughed again, as if they understood each other.

'I've known this tigress for many years,' she said. 'Since she was a cub. Later, I've seen her playing with her own cubs, walking along the riverbank, right over there.'

Jim turned to see the bank of sand, where she pointed, with the flowing water beyond. It was bright daylight but he felt an ominous premonition in the woman's words.

'Two winters ago, when one of the male tigers swam across from Nepal, they mated here in the streambed between the ashram and my farm. All night they roared, shaking the forest with their cries. Her life will soon be over but I feel as if I am tied to her. Last week, she came to the door of this hut and I could hear her breathing, a sound like sand being washed by the waves in the river. Even now, I can feel her presence far away in the forest, waiting in the shade of that rock, licking her wound and tasting the bitter pus on her tongue. The tigress is not afraid. She knows you are following her but her instincts are still sharp, though her strength is waning and she limps when she walks.'

'Will I be able to kill the man-eater tonight?' Jim asked.

'Who knows when her end will come?' Kaiyu's voice was hushed, as if she were speaking to herself instead of answering his question. 'She is hungry. As soon as the shadows begin to darken, she will set off to feed again. If a hunter is waiting for her, she will sense the danger. Her eyesight is clear and she can detect the scent of man on the slightest breeze.'

'Tell me what to do,' said Jim. 'How can I kill her?'

'I told you before,' said Kaiyu. 'She is protected by the goddess who rides upon her back.'

'Then how do I placate the goddess?' Jim asked.

'By offering her something of yourself.'

FOURTEEN

Bimal was leaving the ashram when Jim returned. A group of labourers accompanied him, more than a dozen men carrying bamboo staves and axes, who eyed Jim with suspicion. Further off, the rest of labourers sat waiting at the edge of the streambed, almost three hundred of them altogether.

'They've had enough,' said Bimal. 'We're taking out a protest march, demanding pay and full rations, as well as protection from the tiger. All the labourers, from each of the three camps, are gathering at the Mayaghat rest house.'

'Do you think that's wise?' said Jim.

'What else are they to do, starve to death?' Bimal's tone was adamant and Jim could tell that he had worked himself up for the protest, full of youthful zeal and political conviction. In his white Gandhi cap, he looked as if he'd already won the battle, eyes gleaming with excitement.

'I've located the seventh victim,' said Jim. 'There's a good chance I'll get a shot at the man-eater tonight.'

Mangal Singh, Megh Chand and Khem Chand were watching from beside his tent. He could see the concern in their eyes, knowing the labourers were angry and desperate.

'We can't wait for you to slay the monster,' said Bimal sarcastically. 'We must find our own solution.'

'Kincaid and his men are armed,' said Jim. 'It could easily turn ugly. I would urge you to be patient.'

'When there is injustice and cruelty, who has time for patience?' said Bimal.

'If there's violence, the labourers will be the ones to suffer.'

'Our protest will be non-violent. I have told them that we must restrain ourselves and use passive resistance, even if we are attacked. We must believe in Gandhiji's truth, his message of ahimsa and satyagraha.'

'Do you really think you can control them?' Jim said, aware of the tension in the group of men. Their staves and axes were meant to protect them from the tiger but they could easily be turned to other purposes. Kincaid would find himself outnumbered and probably panic. As soon as he fired, there would be a riot.

'They will control themselves,' said Bimal. 'This will be a peaceful protest.'

'Give me one more night,' said Jim. He then turned to the labourers and spoke to them in Hindustani, explaining that the tigress was likely to return to her kill this evening and he would be there to finish her off. They listened with grim expressions and said nothing in reply.

'You see, the tiger isn't the problem,' said Bimal, also speaking in Hindustani. 'It's British rule. The way you treat these people.'

'How can you be so naive?' said Jim. 'What will they gain from this?'

'Freedom,' said Bimal. 'Dignity.'

'Neither of those words will put food in their stomachs. Why do you think they've come here in the first place?' said Jim. 'They left their villages in Bihar because they were already starving. What will they go back to after your protest is finished?'

'We are only asking for what they were promised,' Bimal answered.

'I'll promise you this,' said Corbett. 'If you hold off for another day or two, I'll kill the man-eater and then I'll go to the Commissioner of Kumaon, who sent me here. I will explain to him what has happened and make sure that every man is paid his due.'

Bimal smiled and shook his head. 'I'm afraid it's too late for that.' Then he raised his fist and shouted, 'Inquilab Zindabad!'

The labourers immediately got to their feet. 'Inquilab Zindabad!'

Jim watched them leave with a sense of foreboding and remorse. Though his sympathies were with the labourers, he could not accept the political rhetoric and posturing of men like Bimal Swadeshi, who used the suffering of others to achieve political ends. At the same time, he hated government officials like Kincaid and everything he represented. More than anything, however, he feared the irrational passions that would lead to chaos and even more suffering.

Sitting by himself, Jim ate his midday meal and spoke only a few words to his men, explaining that they would tie out all three buffaloes tonight before he returned to sit up in the tree.

'Sahib, if there is violence at the rest house,' said Mangal Singh, 'the labourers might come after you. We will stand by you, but there are a thousand of them. They cannot tell one Englishman from another.'

'What are you suggesting?' said Jim.

'Only that you should be careful. This Congresswalla doesn't know where his protests will lead.'

'Let them do what they want,' said Jim. 'We have a job to finish.'

They tied one of the buffaloes near the labour camp, which was deserted now, a foetid mire of mud and tree stumps. The second bait was tethered by the stream between the ashram and Kaiyu's hut. The third, Jim took with him when he set out for the kill in the late afternoon. Halfway there, he found a small rohini tree growing by itself in a sheltered glade. Tying the buffalo to the trunk of the tree so it could browse on the leaves of the lower branches, he continued on his way.

More than ever before, Jim felt a depressing sense of loneliness in the jungle, as if he might never see another person again. Deliberately, he made himself focus on the sounds of the forest, the shrill cries of woodpeckers and the cackle of magpies. But he could not forget the hostility in the labourers' eyes, their anguish and their anger.

It was past four o'clock when he reached the pipal tree and approached the kill. Jim was relieved to see that no scavengers had found it, though a swarm of flies covered the torn flesh on the dead girl's back. She lay exactly as he'd left her but Jim was aware of a change in her face, the smile no longer there and her cheeks swollen, her belly bloating. The corpse seemed to have aged in death, no longer the girl he'd seen this morning but an older woman, raddled beyond her years.

Retreating to the tree, Jim took a ball of twine from his pocket and tied it to his rifle, then started up the tree. The pipal had tendrils braided down the trunk, which was fissured and hollowed out in places so that he could easily make his way up to the branch that overlooked the kill. He wondered if any snakes lived in the tree, for cobras often inhabited a pipal. The leaves looked like a cobra's hood, with thin, long tongues. Hauling the rifle after him, he crawled along the overhanging branch until it forked. Here he found the seat that he was looking for. His feet could be braced on a lower limb with his backside wedged securely on the main branch. It wasn't comfortable but at least there was little risk of falling. Reloading his rifle, he tried to forget everything that had happened that day, the strange conversation with Kaiyu and the hostile crowd of labourers, intent on seeking justice or revenge. Instead, he heard the far-off cry of a serpent eagle, a shrill scream, as it wheeled above the forest in search of prey.

Gradually, evening settled over the Sarda Valley, though it was already dark in the shade of the pipal, its leaves like a green mosaic in which the shapes gradually blurred together until it was impossible to distinguish between foliage and sky. At one point a flock of blossom-headed parakeets arrived, shrieking and chuckling as they fed on the tiny figs that grew amongst the branches. *Ficus religiosa*, Jim recalled the Latin name for pipal, also known as the bodhi tree, under which Gautama Buddha had achieved enlightenment. Somewhere Jim had read how the Buddha later died beneath a sal tree, like those that were being felled at Mayaghat. It seemed to him as if the forest signified a sacred trust between God and man. The first time he set foot within the ring of boulders Jim had sensed something hallowed here and wondered what mysteries the Banrajis assigned to this place.

So far, he had heard no alarm calls. A troop of langurs were feeding on the flowers of a silk-cotton tree a short distance to his right. If the tigress approached from that direction, they would surely warn the rest of the forest. He wondered where the tigress might be and imagined the place that Kaiyu had described—the overhanging rock and flowering vines sheltering the man-eater in her bower.

Moments later, he heard a sound that made him sit upright, a deep thunderous roar from less than half a mile away. The tigress was calling. It began as a moan but grew louder and more resonant as it reached its climax, a volcanic sound that made the hairs on his arms prickle and his mouth go dry. Jim had heard plenty of tigers before but this time there was a distressing note of sadness in the call as well as pain. As he listened, he could tell the tigress was coming towards him. She called nine times and then fell silent.

The girl's body lay below him, forty feet away and slightly to his left. He could raise the rifle to his shoulder without moving anything except his arms. Jim could see the victim's legs crossed at the knees and her torso turned towards him. The shadow of one arm reached up to cover her breast and her neck was thrown back where the tigress's teeth had gripped her throat.

A treepie gave a loud cackle somewhere in the jungle to his right, but he wasn't sure if it was a cry of alarm. For half an hour nothing happened and Jim waited as night closed in. The kill was barely visible and he strained his eyes to catch the slightest hint of movement. Finally, he heard a twig break under the weight of the man-eater's paw. It could have been anything, a rat in the grass, but Jim felt sure the tigress was near. His sixth sense told him she was approaching. The rocks, where the body lay, were a pale white and he could just make out their shapes. If the tigress passed in front of them, he would spot her immediately. Several minutes later, he heard the man-eater breathing and remembered how Kaiyu had described this sound as the river's current lapping at the sand. He knew that she was directly below him, no more than twenty feet away, though beneath the tree it was pitch black. Jim raised the rifle so slowly that his arms ached, then held the heavy weapon to his shoulder. He could hardly see the sights, the twin barrels of the .450/400 receding into darkness.

A few minutes later he heard a shuffling further off, beyond the kill. The tigress had circled round, still out of sight. Another minute passed and his arms were trembling so much, he worried that his bullet would never find its mark. But then the tigress called again from several hundred yards away, moving back up the ridge. The moaning roar conveyed her irritation and anger, as well as the pain that drove her to desperation. Jim knew that she had sensed his presence in the tree and her instinct for self-preservation had trumped her hunger. She would not return tonight.

Another nine hours remained until daylight. Jim was tempted to climb down from his perch and return to his tent but he had no torch or lantern to light his path through the forest. There was always the slim chance the man-eater might come back. Settling himself as best he could, he kept an ear out for telltale sounds. Hours dragged by and he tried to still his mind, though his anxieties about the protest returned, as well as random thoughts about the family properties in Nainital and Maggie's plans to shift uphill from Kaladhungi.

Several times he began to doze off and as he lost consciousness strange dreams seeped into his mind. He found himself in the middle of a mustard field in France, the yellow flowers bright as turmeric and the sky a cobalt blue. He saw two biplanes circling overhead, an aerial dogfight between a German and a British flyer. They swooped and dodged, climbing and wheeling like kites until smoke began to pour out of the British plane and it came towards him, diving steeply before crashing at the edge of the field, and bursting into flames. Jim ran towards the crash site, horrified yet drawn to the disaster. The plane had ploughed a deep trench thirty feet long where the smouldering remains had broken up into scraps of wings and the twisted tail, its rudder hanging by a cable. The whole thing seemed surreal. Peering into the trench, he saw what looked like a shattered coffin, smoke coming up out of the mud.

From behind him he heard a woman's voice speaking a language he couldn't understand. Turning away from the wreckage, he saw the dead girl who lay beneath the tree, though she was alive now, standing waist high in the yellow mustard field, a trace of a smile on her lips, the hand at her naked breast, an image of innocence and grief. She was calling to him but he drew back from her, afraid he would fall into the muddy gash where the shattered remains of the aircraft burned like a fire emerging from the earth.

Jim woke with a start that almost made him fall from the tree. Frantically, he clutched at the rifle and caught his balance in the dark, frightened as much by the dream as the possibility of tumbling headlong from the branch. Though he now forced himself to stay awake, the image continued to haunt his mind, an indelible vision of a nude woman wading towards him through a sea of yellow flowers. Much later, when the pale dawn finally released him from his vigil, he still couldn't erase her from his thoughts.

FIFTEEN

Descending from the pipal tree, Jim felt discouraged, having missed a chance to shoot the man-eater. From the ground below he could see that the seat he'd chosen was too exposed. Foolishly, he had been over-confident and hadn't taken enough precautions. He should have sat closer to the trunk of the tree, which would have shielded his profile and hidden him from view. It would have meant an awkward angle from which to fire but the tigress would not have seen him.

Angry at himself for having wasted an opportunity and knowing that his failure meant the protestors would continue their agitation, Jim made his way back to the rohini tree, where the bait was tied. The buffalo calf lay on the ground complacently, having eaten most of the leaves within reach. Untying the animal, Jim led him down to the streambed fifty yards away and let him drink his fill, before tethering him once more.

There was no trail to follow but he knew the way back to the ashram and recognized landmarks along the route, cutting across the lower edge of the range of hills, then following the largest stream towards the river. It was a beautiful morning but Jim was preoccupied, regretting the squandered opportunity to kill the tigress. Through a gap in the trees he watched a pair of racket-tailed drongos swooping and diving for insects, as if they were playing a game of badminton with an invisible shuttlecock. Yet Jim was in no mood to enjoy the forest and his mind kept going back to the whisper of the man-eater's breathing in the dark and her roar of displeasure as she left her kill untouched. The strange nightmare had also unsettled him and he had trouble detaching his memories from the dream, as if the two had melded in his mind. The dogfight between the two biplanes was something he had witnessed seven years ago in France. The British biplane had been shot down by the German flyer, but it had happened far away from him and he had watched it through field glasses, two specks against the horizon. He remembered feeling distraught and helpless when he saw the aircraft plummet to earth. Jim had been several miles away from the crash site and never saw what was left of the plane.

Eventually, the stream brought him out into the deserted fields above Kaiyu's hut and he cut across to join the path that led to the water's edge, before crossing over to the ashram. It was still early morning and light from the east slanted in across the hills of Nepal, the sun still hidden by clouds. Near the confluence he saw a movement and thought it might be a deer or an otter splashing in the current, but then he saw Kaiyu stand up and lift a water vessel onto her head. The composition of the scene, with a skein of mist over the water was so perfect that Jim dug his camera out of the rucksack and quickly adjusted the focus. By the time he was able to take the first picture, Kaiyu was already halfway up the riverbank and the sun was just breaking through the clouds. Recalibrating the shutter speed, Jim snapped another photograph, then waited for her to come up the trail.

She must have seen him from a distance for she did not seem surprised to find him there. Stopping briefly, one hand steadying the heavy water vessel, she asked, 'What happened last night? I kept waiting for you to shoot.'

'The tigress came but she knew I was there and went away,' said Jim. 'I have no one to blame but myself for having missed a chance.'

'It's not your fault. The tigress will die when her time comes.' She noticed the Rolleiflex in his hands. 'What's that?' she asked.

'A camera,' he said, 'I took your picture, coming up from the river.'

She laughed, as if it were an absurd thing to do, then turned and headed on up the trail. Packing the camera away in its case, Jim followed her. By the time she set the water vessel down, the sun was fully out. Some of the water had splashed on Kaiyu's shoulder wetting her sari and blouse.

'I've never had my photo taken before,' she said. 'Can you show it to me?'

'Right now, I can't. The picture is still inside the camera. Only when I get back to Nainital will I be able to have it developed and printed. Then I'll send you a copy.'

'How does it keep the picture inside?' she asked.

Jim began to explain but Kaiyu seemed distracted and he could tell she wasn't listening. After a minute, she said, 'I'll make some tea.'

He watched her go into the hut and heard the sound of a pan being placed on the hearth and water pouring from the vessel. The fire was already lit and smoke was filtering through the slate roof. When she came out, Kaiyu looked at him with a serious expression. Lighting two cigarettes with the same match he handed one to her.

'Today, I am going to the rest house to see what's happening,' she said, inhaling the smoke. 'I promised Bimal I would join his protest.'

'It could be dangerous,' said Jim. 'There's bound to be trouble.'

'That man, Kincaid, is vicious, but underneath he is a coward. He will run away when he sees their resolve.'

Jim shook his head. 'I had hoped to kill the tigress last night and put an end to this. But I failed.'

He stared at her with a defeated expression, the empty rifle resting beside him and his hat upon his knee. Drawing on the cigarette, he coughed and looked away.

'The tigress has outwitted me,' he said, disheartened. 'You were right. She knows I am hunting her and she is more cunning and careful than before.'

'But you are a patient shikari,' she said. 'How many days have you waited to kill other tigers in the past?'

'Sometimes a month or more,' Jim admitted. 'And other times, I've had to wait a year before I got a chance.'

'Then why are you discouraged?' she said. 'You've hardly been here for a week, no more...'

'It seems much longer,' he said in a dejected voice. 'Last night I was sure the man-eater would come to the kill, but I should have known...'

Kaiyu watched him without speaking as he stared at the elephant hill where the early morning light had struck the trees and glowed against the shadows beyond, as if the light came from within the mountain, shining like a buried star.

The two of them smoked in silence, until Kaiyu tossed her cigarette aside and entered the hut. Jim watched one of the chickens scratching at a pile of leaves that she had swept aside from the area around the hut. Off in the distance he heard the drumming of a hornbill's wings.

'Sahibji,' he heard Kaiyu call, 'your tea is ready.'

Jim crushed the stub of his cigarette on a stone beside him and got up, puzzled that she hadn't brought the tea outside.

He stooped to enter the narrow doorway and saw a layer of smoke suspended beneath the exposed rafters of the roof. The only light came from the hearth, where flames rustled in the dark. As his eyes adjusted, Jim saw Kaiyu standing to one side, away from the fire. She had unwrapped her sari and he could see the contours of her slender body in the shadows of the hut. For a moment, he almost stepped back into the sunlight, afraid of himself as much as her. But she reached out and drew him gently into her embrace.

SIXTEEN

Mangal Singh had cooked a simple meal of potatoes and dal, placing two rotis folded together on one side of the enamel plate, as well as a sliced onion and a green chilli. As usual, Jim ate very little but he was grateful for the food. Sitting outside his tent he chewed it slowly, the sharpness of the chilli burning his tongue.

Kaiyu had set off for Mayaghat on her own, though he had tried to persuade her not to go. She seemed determined to add her voice to the protest. As Jim thought back on their lovemaking, he felt an unfamiliar sense of contentment. Whatever had taken place between them seemed part of the natural order of things. His fears about the protest and his discouragement at having missed his chance to kill the tigress no longer weighed on his mind. This was not the first time he'd lain with a woman but Kaiyu's touch had calmed him in a way he'd never known before. The shared intimacy of their physical desires had helped him replenish a part of himself that he had lost sometime ago, perhaps during the war, maybe later following his mother's death. From the first moment he'd seen Kaiyu, Jim had found himself drawn to her. For all her talk of spirits and magic, he knew she wasn't a witch but simply a woman who lived alone in the forest because of the circumstances of her life. And yet like him, she needed the solace of another's hand upon her breast and the innocent pleasure of two bodies entwined like a slip knot cinching tighter and tighter before pulling free.

That afternoon, Jim slept soundly for a couple of hours and woke rested and alert. Khem Chand greeted him as he emerged from his tent with news that the tigress had killed one of the buffaloes near the timber camp. He and his brother had gone to give it fodder and water when they discovered that the tigress had broken the rope and dragged the buffalo calf into the forest.

Quickly Jim got ready and they were on their way within twenty minutes, heading across the stream and into the forest. Both brothers accompanied him, Khem Chand carrying Jim's rucksack and Megh Chand the 12-bore. Rested and with his mind at ease, Jim felt a renewed sense of purpose. He hoped that he would soon have another opportunity to kill the tigress. This time he was determined not to fail.

But when they reached the spot where the buffalo had been tethered and followed the drag marks into the jungle, he began to have misgivings. The buffalo had been carried for three-quarters of a mile into a deep gully that lay between two ridges, thickly wooded with trees. By the time they found the remains, Jim was convinced that the tigress hadn't made this kill. She was too old and crippled to have dragged the buffalo this far, over difficult ground. The pugmarks of a large male tiger confirmed that it was the man-eater's grown cub, not the tigress herself.

Khem Chand and Megh Chand were not convinced. They felt sure it was the man-eater, but Jim showed them the difference in the prints, how the right foot had no injuries and the strength it must have taken to drag the buffalo's carcass up into the gully over rocks and boulders. Only the hindquarters had been eaten but Jim knew with certainty that it would be a waste of time for him to sit up over this kill.

By now, shadows were lengthening and they retraced their steps to the deserted lumber camp. From here Jim told his men to go directly back to the ashram, as he set off for the pipal tree once more. When he reached the clearing, he saw two jackals skulking nearby, and knew that scavengers had found the kill. The stench of decomposing flesh tainted the stagnant air. Jim could hear the buzzing of flies. He did not bother to examine the body but climbed straight into the tree and wedged himself and his rucksack between the main trunk and the branch he'd sat upon the night before. The kill was visible from this angle but only the victim's legs and her back.

It was already five o'clock. A couple of crows were in the trees nearby. After a while, they descended and picked at the remains. The jackals returned as well, slinking out of the bushes and tearing at the flesh with their teeth. Jim wondered whether the tigress would return tonight. As it grew darker, a stillness came over the jungle, as if suddenly every form of life had retreated. The only sound that Jim could hear was the pulse of his own heartbeat.

And then, like a shadowy mirage, the tigress appeared. There was no warning, not even the snap of a twig. But he suddenly saw her standing broadside between him and the kill. Just enough light remained for Jim to make out the black calligraphy of stripes and tawny fur, the curved tail that swayed behind her. The .450/400 lay across his lap. He lifted it slowly and pivoted in his seat. Before he could fully extend the rifle, he had to raise his left arm over the rucksack without dislodging it. His breathing seemed to stop as the sights lined up with the tigress's shoulder. The range was no more than fifty yards and she was looking away from him. But as he finally got the rifle in position, and put his finger to the trigger, the tigress turned.

He saw her eyes staring at him for an instant before he fired, as if with a look of recognition. The explosion was like a hammer striking an anvil and the rifle kicked Jim's shoulder with a vicious recoil. At the same moment, he heard the smack of the bullet and saw the tigress spring forward, disappearing into the night. Silence returned and Jim's ears were ringing. He kept the rifle ready for several minutes before he lowered the weapon. His hands were shaking and he felt sick to his stomach. There was no question his bullet had struck the man-eater but he couldn't tell if she was dead or wounded. Jim knew it would be suicidal to descend in the dark and he resigned himself to another long night in the tree.

Once his nerves had settled, he felt a sense of detachment. The silence and darkness of the jungle seemed part of a separate world. He was there alone within himself. He could no longer smell the rotting corpse and felt invisible. Thinking of Kaiyu, he wondered what was happening at the rest house but none of that seemed to matter any more. Hours later, sleep came upon him and once when he awoke Jim felt as if someone was sitting beside him, a man or a woman he wasn't sure. He thought it might be Kaiyu, though they didn't speak and he felt no need to question her. But then he slept again and next when he opened his eyes he was alone.

Finally, the sky began to change, as he saw the stars disappear beyond the pattern of pipal leaves. The air had grown colder and when the light came, he could see mist all around him. His eyes scanned the rocks where the body lay for any sign of the tigress but Jim could see nothing and he forced himself to wait until he could distinguish one leaf from another.

Sliding down the tree, he quickly retrieved his rifle and slipped two bullets into the chambers. Snapping shut the breech he released the safety catch with his thumb. He knew in which direction the tigress had gone and made his way around the base of the tree with the .450/400 at his shoulder. There was no need to search for blood or pugmarks. After stepping away from the tree, Jim moved out of the shadows, the grey light filtering in from above. Curtains of mist obscured the trees beyond. Another few feet and Jim saw the tigress.

She was lying against a rock, with her back to him. Though he knew she was dead, he picked up a pebble and threw it at her. The man-eater didn't move and he went forward, the rifle now at his waist but a finger still on the trigger.

His bullet had struck her in the ribs on the left flank and ruptured her heart. The final lunge to escape was nothing but a reflex for she must have been dead before she hit the ground. He could see the festering wound on her right shoulder, where the skin had been torn away. The exposed flesh had a soapy appearance because of the infection. Her mouth was open and he could see one canine broken and her gums blackened with age. The fur, when he touched it, was dry and brittle. Even in the dawn light, he could tell there was no point in skinning this tiger as a trophy. She already looked as if she had been tacked up on a wall for twenty years, bald patches on her legs.

Jim put his rifle down and sat on a rock to have a smoke. He felt no sense of victory, only a mild satisfaction at having finally completed the task he'd set for himself, as well as regret that the tigress had suffered so much and caused so much suffering in turn. Just as he was about to throw his cigarette aside, he heard what sounded like a voice and then a skittering in the leaves.

The mist cloaked the forest in a damp grey shroud but he saw leaves move and moments later a figure emerged. It was one of the Banraji hunters, followed by another, and then another, until eight of them stood in the clearing. They carried bows and arrows as well as spears but their faces showed no aggression. One of them acknowledged Jim with a hesitant gesture of his hand but the others ignored him. Their eyes were fixed on the tigress.

Coming nearer, they crouched and touched her. One man lifted a paw and extended the claws, feeling their sharpness. Another stroked her tail. Each of them had probably seen this tigress before and recognized her from when she was a healthy mother, leading her cubs through the forest and teaching them to hunt. While their faces showed little emotion, they seemed to mourn her passing.

After a few minutes, they cut down two saplings and stripped vines from trees nearby to use as ropes. By now the light was brighter and Jim took out his camera, so that he could get a picture of the tigress. He pointed for the Banrajis to sit around her and told them he wanted their photograph. Whether they understood what he meant he couldn't be sure but the hunters crouched beside the man-eater, staring at him with sombre expressions.

None of them spoke or asked his permission to carry her away. But without hesitation they lashed the tigress's paws to the saplings and lifted her, all eight of them together, shouldering her weight. Jim did not try to stop the hunters, but let the Banrajis carry the man-eater into the mist and trees, bearing her off through the forest.

SEVENTEEN

For the first time since he had arrived at Mayaghat, Jim could let down his
guard. The danger was now gone but also the constant pressure to
find the man-eater. With the rucksack on his shoulders and the rifle
tucked into the crook of his arm, he headed back to the ashram,
alive to the bird calls around him, the gnarled shapes of termite
castles and the furtive gaze of a leopard cat that happened to cross
his path. The animal stopped for several seconds before bounding
into the underbrush. Seeing this small predator, no more than three
feet long but with a splendid coat, he felt as much elation as though
he'd come upon another tiger. For the rodents, reptiles and birds on
which it fed, the leopard cat must have seemed a ferocious monster,
though Jim could tell this timid creature viewed him as a blundering
giant, representing danger and destruction.

His men had heard the report of the rifle from over two miles
away, for sounds carry across hills and valleys. Jim could see the
relief on their faces when he told them the tigress was dead. After
a mug of tea, he went down to the river and washed, lingering in
the current as long as he could bear the cold, then changing into
a clean shirt, shorts and socks, so that for a few moments at least
he felt civilized again.

Jim was already thinking of the long trek home. He would
send his sister a telegram from Tanakpur. By the time he reached
Kaladhungi, Maggie would have packed up the house, ready to move
back uphill to Nainital.

As he returned to his tent, he caught sight of a line of men
coming up the valley, ten or twelve of the labourers. Immediately,
his sense of contentment was replaced by uncertainty when he

saw they were carrying a bier. Mangal Singh and the others had noticed the procession too. They stopped whatever they were doing and watched the group make its way single file along the edge of the trees and down an overgrown path that brought them to the ashram gate. Without stopping, the solemn group of men walked past Jim and went around the ruined temple then placed the body on the ground.

As the men went by him, Jim saw Kaiyu's face, partly covered, her lifeless features framed by lank strands of hair. Going closer, he was aware of the labourers' eyes upon him, resentment and suspicion in their gaze. But the sudden shock of seeing Kaiyu laid out on a bamboo bier, and the bloodstains on her sari, took the breath from his lungs. One of her hands lay at her side and he could see her fingers clenched as if she were holding something. Kaiyu looked much smaller in death, a fragile husk of herself. Dazed and distraught, Jim kneeled by the bier, recalling her laughter from the day before, her chiding voice, her fingers combing the hair at the back of his neck. He drew the corner of the sari away from her face and saw her sightless eyes staring back at him.

Bimal Swadeshi was among the group of men, though Jim hadn't registered his presence until he finally looked up. At the same moment, Khem Chand stepped forward and lifted Jim by the arm and drew him aside. He then faced the labourers and announced that the man-eater was dead, telling them the Sahib had killed the tiger the night before. The danger was gone. Through a haze of emotions, Jim realized that his men were afraid that the labourers might attack him. Gathering himself together, he looked around and saw the first signs of relief in the labourers' features as they absorbed the news of the man-eater's death.

Bimal looked at him with a sceptical expression then spoke in Hindi. 'Is it true?'

'Yes,' Jim replied. 'The man-eater is no more. There is nothing to fear.' Then he looked across at Kaiyu's body again. 'What happened?' he asked.

'Kincaid shot her,' said Bimal.

'But why? How could this happen?' Jim asked.

'Last evening, we had been sitting in protest outside the rest house for more than twenty-four hours,' Bimal explained, speaking in English now. 'Kincaid ordered the forest guards to fire on the crowd and disperse us. The guards knew what would happen and they were afraid. Kincaid shouted but they refused. Then the DFO grabbed a shotgun from one of his men and pointed it at me, saying he would shoot me first. All at once, I heard Kaiyu's voice calling out from the other side. She was sitting with the other women, about thirty feet from the bungalow, and got up and began taunting him. By this time it was already dark and we had lit fires to keep warm. She stepped into the firelight, pointing her finger and telling him to go back to England where he belonged. I wanted to warn her but she stood there unafraid and laughed at him, as if it were a joke.'

Bimal's voice broke as he said this and he paused to collect himself before he continued.

'Kincaid fired both barrels, one after the other. The pellets struck her in the chest and she fell back into the crowd. At first, there was panic and people began to run. One or two of the forest guards fired their guns over our heads. Suddenly, the crowd turned around and surged towards the rest house. By this time Kincaid had run back to the quarters. In the confusion, I saw him getting onto his horse, with a revolver in his hand, firing twice before he rode away. The forest guards ran off too. I tried to calm the protestors but their anger was too great, nothing could stop them. They burned the rest house and looted the quarters where the rations were kept. It was chaos,' said Bimal. 'They took burning logs from the fire and threw them into the windows of the bungalow. Smoke was everywhere and in the darkness you could see only flames coming out of the building. When I finally reached Kaiyu, she was already dead.'

While Bimal spoke to Jim, the labourers drew back and squatted in the shade of the mango tree, as if they had fulfilled whatever task they'd been assigned. Jim shook his head and waved a hand in a helpless gesture.

'I told her not to go,' he said.

'If it wasn't for her, I would be dead,' said Bimal. 'Kincaid was going to shoot me. She saved my life.'

'It seems so senseless,' said Jim, 'so utterly senseless.'

For a minute or more they were silent.

'Where is the tigress?' Bimal asked.

Jim stared at him, as if he didn't understand the question.

'The Banrajis,' he said at last. 'They took her away.'

'These men will want proof that the tiger is dead,' said Bimal.

'What difference does it make any more?' said Jim.

For the first time, he noticed the soot and blood on Bimal's clothes, how his hair was singed and the look of desolation in his eyes. Stepping past him, Jim approached the group of labourers and explained that he would guide them to the girl's body and help them recover her remains. By now, the anger had left them and they seemed ordinary men whose lives had been a struggle since birth, driven by hunger and poverty, debt and humiliation. Whoever they were, these men seemed lost in the forest, as silent and innocent as the trees they had felled.

⁂

Later in the day, as the sun descended, Jim sat alone by the river and watched the pyres being built. By this time the Banrajis had heard of Kaiyu's death and a group of them had come down from the elephant hill. In silence they helped carry her body onto the sand. Gathering driftwood, the hunters constructed her pyre, stacking the logs and branches around Kaiyu's body. For a moment Jim thought it looked like a funeral barge that would bear her downstream. When the flames began to dance, the hunters moved back while the two plumes of smoke spun together on the breeze, spilling out above the current of the river, unfurling like the tangled memories of a dream.

EIGHTEEN

*Many forest-dwelling cultures share a belief that every human being
has a counterpart in nature, with whom his or her fate is
linked. For instance, the American Indian, we are told, takes
on the names of bears or wolves, eagles or bison, because these
are companion creatures with whom he shares a soul. In a
similar manner, people in Africa are often possessed by the
spirits of wild animals, like lions or leopards, who give them
courage and strength, cunning and guile. Here in India too
we have the same kind of stories, where a mystical affinity
exists between beast and man. In our modern wisdom, we call
these primitive beliefs, suggesting ignorance and superstition.
However, anyone who has walked through a forest at dawn and
heard the chorus of bird calls and watched the jungle come
to life can be in no doubt that we share a vital connection
with other species.*

*Recently, I was asked to hunt down a man-eater in the Sarda
Valley, near a place called Mayaghat, where the depredations of
this tigress terrorized gangs of labourers engaged in felling the
forest. I am hesitant to tell this story because my readers may
think that I am promoting unscientific theories and political
sentiments that should be kept in check. But in the end this
experience has taught me more about humanity than either
politics or science...*

Jim had been writing for several hours now and he had filled half
a dozen sheets of foolscap with the tracery of his words. Yet he felt
as if he still hadn't begun his story and these were prefatory lines,

which he would cross out in a later draft. He flipped back and revised an earlier paragraph, cutting phrases...

> If you asked someone to choose the kind of death that he or she would prefer, very few, if any, would want to be killed by a tiger. And yet it is quick and relatively painless. Tigers do not torture their victims or prolong the suffering. Their teeth puncture your throat, cutting off your breathing instantly, as a swift jerk of the predator's head snaps your neck. Unlike a hanging or death by guillotine, there is none of the prolonged agony of anticipation that accompanies those forms of execution. Instead, a tiger takes you by surprise and before you know it the deed is done, quick as a bullet. Whatever pain a tiger inflicts lasts only a second or two, no more.
>
> As I write these words, I cannot help but think of a brave woman I met in the Sarda Valley, who lived alone in the forest, tending a small farm and collecting wild herbs in the forest. Though the man-eater had taken several victims from the labour camps nearby and came sniffing at her door, she was not frightened but seemed to possess an uncanny knowledge of this tigress as if they had known each other in a previous life...

Setting his pen aside, Jim stared out the window of his daftar at Gurney House. Though Maggie called it his study, he always spoke of it as his daftar, an office or workroom, full of receipt books and files, the inevitable paperwork and clutter of being a landlord. Whenever he had a chance to write, Jim would push the piles of ledgers aside and take out loose sheets of foolscap that he preferred over notebooks or journals. He wrote using a fountain pen with a clear, flowing hand. Even before he finished a sentence, Jim began crossing out words and changing adjectives or metaphors. Only after he had completed several drafts and made a clean copy would he show it to Maggie, who was his harshest critic but also a shrewd editor.

Robin lay at Jim's feet beneath the desk, dreaming of chasing monkeys, both front and back paws kicking as he emitted soft, whimpering barks in his sleep.

It was early evening in Nainital. Through his office window, Jim could see a honeysuckle trellis in the garden, beyond which rose the shadowy profiles of the hills surrounding the silver mirror of the lake. An octave owl was calling somewhere in the oaks at the edge of the yard. Jim had lit the bukhari because it was still cold in early April after the sun went down.

Shuffling through the papers on his desk, he found the envelopes from Hazlett's Studio containing the prints and negatives they had developed for him. Jim took out the set of pictures from Mayaghat and studied the image of Kaiyu coming up the riverbank with a water vessel on her head. He could almost see her body moving, though she seemed farther away than he remembered, a distant figure dwarfed by the surrounding forest. Flipping ahead through the stack of pictures, he saw the Banrajis posing with the tigress, their serious, sombre faces staring into the camera as if it were an unknown window into an unseen world. The old tigress seemed indifferent to those around her, eyes open even in death.

The other set of pictures were those he had taken from the machan above the Baur Canal before he'd set off to hunt the man-eater. Of these, two prints pleased him more than the others. The young male tiger stood facing the camera, looking up at the tree in which Jim sat. The focus, aperture and shutter speed had been perfectly synchronized so that every hair on the tiger was visible and the stripes on his face and shoulders stood out in bold contrast to the lighter sections of his coat

Yesterday, as soon as he brought the photographs home, Jim showed them to Maggie with excitement, as if he'd carried in a trophy from the jungle. She exclaimed with delight when she saw the picture of the tiger.

'Why, he looks as if he's posing for a portrait!' she said, holding it up to the light.

But when she saw her own photograph, sitting on the veranda at Kaladhungi with Robin beside her, she was disapproving.

'You've turned me into an old maid,' she complained.

'This one's not so bad,' Jim said.

'No, I've got my eyes half-closed,' she said. 'And that foolish smile's not very becoming.'

He then showed her the photographs from Mayaghat, pictures of the fish he'd caught and the Banrajis carrying the boar. When Maggie saw the photograph of Kaiyu bringing water from the river, she stopped and cocked her head. 'It's a beautiful place,' she said. 'I wish I'd gone with you.'

The next photograph was one he'd taken of Kaiyu standing outside her hut, preparing to leave for the protest. Jim had snapped the picture on an impulse, without warning her, and there was a startled look of amusement on her face as the camera caught her by surprise. The hand she'd raised to drape her sari across one shoulder was blurred but the rest of the picture was in focus.

'Who's she?' Maggie asked.

'A village woman,' Jim said, not wanting to say any more as Maggie studied the photograph.

'She seems so happy,' his sister said. 'It's wonderful how poor people can be content with their lives.'

Jim was about to reply but stopped himself as Maggie handed the pictures back and went off to prepare their tea.

Now, as he sat at his desk, he stared at the picture again. Selecting a cigarette from a tin on his desk he lit it, tossing the match into an ashtray containing half a dozen butts which had been stubbed out since he sat down to write. Jim remembered watching Kaiyu as she smoked and wondered if she had been as happy as Maggie supposed. The smoke in his lungs caused an ache inside his ribs that he couldn't expel even when he exhaled.

Picking up the sheets of paper on which he'd begun to write his story, Jim read over the words. This time he didn't reach for his pen to change a spelling or correct a phrase. He simply read through the paragraphs as the cigarette smouldered between his lips. When he finally finished, Jim sat for a while and listened to the owl outside, whistling two notes, each of them an octave apart. Deliberately, he stood up, holding the foolscap pages covered with writing. Opening the front of the bukhari he peered inside at the burning logs before consigning his words to the flames.

III

UNTIL THE DAY BREAK
1953

Six years ago, in 1947, my sister Maggie and I set sail from India and moved to the Central Highlands of Kenya. The town of Nyeri where we have settled lies at 5,750 feet above sea level, roughly a thousand feet lower than Nainital. Along with a close friend, Percy Wyndham, former Commissioner of Kumaon, I have invested in a coffee plantation. This provides some income and distraction but allows me enough time to indulge in wildlife photography, which has replaced my lifelong passion for hunting.

On a number of recent occasions people have asked me why I chose to leave India and settle in Kenya, especially during the waning years of my life. It is a question I have often asked myself and for which there is no simple answer, if, in fact, there can be any answer at all. Why would someone willingly leave his birthplace to start a new life far away from everything that he has known and loved and sought to make his own? For seventy-two years, India was my home. The forests and mountains of Kumaon are as familiar to me as the sunburnt skin on the back of my hand. Departing India was one of the most difficult decisions I have ever faced, uprooting myself from the soil in which three generations of my family are buried; leaving behind the swift waters and still lakes in which I was baptized by nature's benevolent currents and calming depths; forsaking the jungles which provided me unlimited adventures and stories; turning my back on so many good people who trusted me with their lives and offered loyalty and friendship beyond words.

The easiest answer, of course, is politics. As India's new leaders struggled to forge their independence in the years leading up to 1947, it became clear to me that I was no longer welcome amidst the clamour of speeches and slogans. Many of my Indian friends tried to assure me that nothing would change and it was all posturing and rhetoric. For the sake of the poorest in India, I hope that isn't true. Much needs to change before their lives become any easier and promises made in the quest for freedom must be kept.

But as the British Empire pulled up its tent pegs and struck camp to head home, I realized that there would be anger and resentment towards my race. The white man has given India many things of great value but he has also taken far more than his share and, in many cases, imposed unjust prejudices and priorities on people who have lived under the yoke of foreign domination for nearly a century and a half. Whatever reprisals occur might not take the extreme forms of violence that erupted in 1857, when my grandfather and other family members were slaughtered during the Mutiny. Nevertheless, if politics spills into the streets it is a scourge that turns friends into adversaries, reducing human behaviour to a brute contest in which all rules are abandoned and there can be no victor, only the vanquished. Some journalists have described it as the 'law of the jungle', which is an odious comparison, for in the absence of man, most jungles exist in peaceful harmony, governed by laws of nature and the eternal, equitable balance between life and death.

One of the first moments when I realized that sooner or later I would be forced to leave India was in the spring of 1932, when I had gone fishing along the upper reaches of the Ramganga River, a three-day trek from Nainital. It had been a dry winter. Already, in March, the forests had turned to tinder, especially plantations of chir pines, which the forest department cultivates for resin and timber. Camped on the riverbank, we had a clear view of the mountains above us but, by the second day, a haze had settled over the valley and I knew it was smoke. All night we could see fires burning across the ridges, distant scribbles of flame like bright dragons crawling up the mountains. Though we were miles away, it was unnerving and depressing to think of all that would be lost, the nests of birds igniting and the suffocating smoke killing off a whole generation of wildlife, insects, reptiles and plants.

And yet the full significance of those fires didn't strike me until I learned they had been lit deliberately in protest. The idea that people would set the jungle ablaze because they were hostile to the government seemed a senseless and desperate act. Of course, I understood the history behind those flames, how the original forests had been felled and replaced by commercial timber, how people who had lived in the jungle for centuries were treated as criminals simply because they were using the forests as their ancestors had done before them. All of that, I know, was part of the incendiary process. Nevertheless, as I watched those ribbons of fire reducing the mountains to charred wastelands of ash, I felt an overwhelming sense of anger and alienation, as if something of myself were being destroyed.

For nearly a week I watched the foothills burn, and whatever pleasure I got from our days by the river was erased by the destruction we witnessed. Fire, of course, is an integral part of nature, but in the hands of man it becomes a symbol of abomination. Sitting at night in the darkness of the Ramganga Valley and watching those fires creep up the mountains, I knew that I would have to seek new pastures.

Walking back to Nainital, we passed through several forests that had been decimated by flames. Blackened tree trunks still smouldered and the air was heavy with smoke. On the crest of one ridge lay a village that had been spared by the fire, though some fields had burned. Three men were sitting in the shade of an apricot tree. When I asked them who had lit the fire, they looked blankly at me, as if I were a fool not to understand. 'What does it matter how the fire started?' one of them said, with a note of accusation in his voice. 'The question is, who will put it out?'

Maggie was already resigned to our departure from India, though she never insisted that we leave and allowed me to make the decision myself. Many of our English friends and acquaintances were preparing to go home. Most of them had property and family in England to which they would return. They invited us to settle near them but neither Maggie nor I relished a quiet life in the Midlands, or Sussex, or wherever it was in Ireland that our ancestors came from.

'The climate won't suit us,' Maggie would say. 'We need a warmer, brighter place, closer to the equator.'

I understood what she meant, though her impressions of England came mostly from novels, the damp and gloomy heaths of *Wuthering*

Heights and the poisonous London fog that Dickens describes with melancholy eloquence. During our last decade in India, my health had deteriorated, with recurring attacks of malaria and an abscess in my ear that could have killed me. We both wanted dry, fresh air and sunshine.

'I can't imagine you huddled by a gas fire knitting woollen stockings to keep yourself warm,' I joked with her. 'We should go to East Africa instead.'

Maggie looked at me with a sceptical expression. I had been to Kenya once already and liked the place, as well as the people.

'So, you'll shoot lions now, instead of tigers?' she said.

'No,' I said. 'But I hear that a Nile perch, pound for pound, puts up as much fight as a mahseer.'

And so, without much discussion or argument between us, it was agreed that we would sell our house in Nainital, as well as the few other properties that remained, and move to Africa, going on the final adventure of our lives.

꘏

Kenya is an astonishingly beautiful country with an abundance of wildlife. No other place on earth comes closer to deserving the title of the 'happy hunting grounds'. These open savannahs and highlands are entirely different from the jungles of my youth. Standing on a hillock overlooking a grass-covered plain, I can see more animals at once than I would have observed in a year of tramping through the forests of India. And the variety of species is far greater too, with dozens of different antelope—from the diminutive duiker to magnificent eland and kudu. The cheetah has disappeared in India, exterminated by hunters and agriculturalists alike, but it is still alive and well on the African plain, one of many predators who feed on a multitude of creatures that populate this plentiful Eden.

A few weeks ago, accompanying friends on safari, I walked out into the grasslands of Tsavo, and spent a pleasant morning alone with my camera. By the time I returned to my tent, I had exposed four reels of film. Each frame contained a different species, from giraffe to hyenas, impala and warthogs. More remarkable than that, these wild creatures permitted an old man to wander in peace, though I was careful not to intrude on their pathways and gave a rhinoceros wide berth. The elephants could easily have trampled me, as might the Cape buffalo. And the lions of Tsavo, who have a reputation for man-eating, had the perfect opportunity to add a human entrée to their menu. Yet nothing untoward occurred and I was permitted to go on living for the time being, despite moving more slowly now and limping because of old wounds.

Not far from here, in the Olduvai Gorge, Dr Louis Leakey, the noted palaeontologist, has unearthed remains of our earliest cousins. His recent discoveries have turned a new chapter on the understanding of human ancestry. This region of East Africa, in the remote Rift Valley, is now being hailed as the cradle of evolution. The stone tools and weapons disinterred with painstaking care reveal ancient hominids who first stalked this land. Fragments of bones have been recovered and pieced together like a puzzle that offers enticing answers to the mystery of our creation. What has emerged from the Olduvai Gorge is a creature we recognize as being an inherent part of ourselves, a primitive hunter, half-animal and half-man, yet indivisibly a member of our extended family, whose ape-like anatomy resembles our own.

As I stepped out onto the vast savannahs of Tsavo, I could easily imagine myself being one of those prehistoric bipeds taking its first furtive steps across the abundant plain and seeing limitless herds of game. The earliest hunters to walk this land were easy prey, even as they quickly honed their predatory skills. Coming down from the trees was not an easy transformation for our ancestors, leaving behind a plentiful diet of fruit and leaves for obvious dangers awaiting them on the ground. But something in us stirs to the chase! Even as we fear the leopard and the lion, we emulate their cunning and patient guile. Over centuries, man has become a hunter by nature and we have developed into one of the most successful killers on earth, not only of other species but of our own kind as well. Though we may have acquired the accoutrements of civilization, along the way we have also picked up traits that are despicable and loathsome. The dark history of the last decade, with mounting evidence of Hitler's depravity, offers proof enough of this, as does the looming shadow of Stalin's red armies.

꙳

In the course of an eventful and varied life, I have seen supposedly civilized men behaving in abominable ways. At the same time, I have witnessed acts of great dignity and honour performed by people who live in the jungle. The inequalities of our society are greater now than ever before, yet history will record only the superficial advances of mankind rather than a continuing and unconscionable failure to lift our fellow human beings out of poverty and despair. In this regard the twentieth century is no better than the nineteenth and I doubt very much that anything will change, even after the turn of the next millennium. Humanity is a deceptive noun that suggests our best qualities as a species, though it often masks prejudice and inequity.

In 1917, as I have written elsewhere, I volunteered to take a labour force to Europe from India to assist with what has been dubbed the 'Great War'. Five hundred courageous men from the villages of Kumaon travelled with me all the way across the kala pani, risking not only their lives but future incarnations as well, for it is often said that Hindus who go abroad forsake their caste and creed. From England, where we first landed, my men and I were sent to France. Posted safely behind the front lines, our 70th Kumaon Labour Corps assisted in building roads and trenches as well as barracks and even a makeshift airfield. It has been the proudest achievement of my life to lead those five hundred men to war and return home with all of them alive, except one.

When I think back on that experience and recall the loyalty and dedication of those men who trusted me enough to leave their homes and families for the battlefields of Europe, it seems remarkable that human beings are capable of such sacrifices, especially for an unknown cause. Yet I often wonder what those men must have thought. Until we boarded the train from Kathgodam to Bombay, most of them had never travelled outside the hills. The only landscapes they knew were forested mountains and terraced fields, the hardship of ploughing rocky soil and waiting for rain to fall and irrigate meagre crops. Their homes were thatch huts and the only source of warmth and light was a simple clay hearth. Almost all of them were illiterate and none spoke English. Most had never buttoned a shirt before or buckled a belt. Yet they put on their uniforms bravely and set off to fight another man's war. They carried shovels and pickaxes rather than rifles but these were the arms they proudly bore.

We were fortunate to be spared the German guns or the mustard gas and bayonets. Most of our time was spent in mundane chores, hauling loads and building drains, while others carried out bloodier tasks. For a while our camp was near Artois, where battle lines hadn't moved a hundred yards, this way or that, for the past two years. Yellow fields of rape grew nearby and the men recognized the flowers and picked the fresh mustard leaves to cook with potatoes, the way they did at home. I often visited the mess tent where the Kumaonis prepared their simple meals. (They got the same rations as the rest of us but didn't know what to do with tins of bacon and corned beef.) Often, I ate with them, accepting a plate of rice and dal. Those familiar spices and flavours took us home to the mountains we had left behind. One night, as I was sitting outside the mess tent with a mug of tea, we heard the far-off rumble of howitzers and one of the men asked if it was thunder. I almost lied to keep his spirits up, but then I thought better of it and told him these were German cannons.

'Will their bullets reach us here?' he asked me.

'No,' I said, speaking Hindustani. 'Those guns are eight miles away. It would take us a full day to march within range of the Germans.'

He thought this over for a moment. 'Do you think we'll ever see any Germans?' he asked. 'And how will we recognize them, if we do?'

'They probably look no different from me,' was the answer I gave. 'Our uniforms are the only thing that sets us apart.'

'So, they're sahibs like you?' he asked, bewildered.

We could see distant flashes and phosphorescent flares against the night sky, where the fighting raged on. By next morning the guns had fallen silent and there was an eerie quiet at dawn. I am used to hearing bird calls announce the sunrise but here there were none. The faint smell of chlorine lingered on the breeze, though it was so diffused it would do us no harm. Then off in the distance I heard a drum. Soon all the men were up and we watched reinforcements march by, an Irish regiment, with the officers on horseback and young men stepping out smartly along the highway that we had just repaired. One of the officers stopped and asked who we were, puzzled to see so many brown faces amidst the mustard fields of France. When I told him my men were from Kumaon, in the foothills of the Himalayas, he looked perplexed.

'Oh, Indians,' he said. 'Good show! Have you brought any tigers or elephants along? We'll set them loose on the Boche!'

For the next two days we continued to fill potholes on the road, a boring but necessary task. After nightfall we listened to the bombardment beyond the horizon. On the third night, I was suddenly awakened by two of my men, who said a message had arrived from the front. When I got up to see who it was, a dispatch rider handed me our marching orders. We were to pack up and move forward at dawn.

I had no idea what was expected of us but we obeyed. An hour after sunrise our labour corps set off, the men marching behind me carrying their kit bags with shovels and picks on their shoulders. Four hours later, we arrived at a field station, about a mile from the front, where I reported to the officer in charge. He was in the midst of studying maps and troop placements with his staff. For an awkward moment, he had no idea who I was or why we were there. Finally, it dawned on him.

'Ah, the *coolies!*' he said, with an impatient wave of his hand. 'We need you to lay out a cemetery and dig us some graves. Rutherford will show you where.'

I saluted and followed the young lieutenant out of the tent. He wasn't more than nineteen and I could tell he was shaken by what he'd seen so far, speaking in a soft stammer as he pointed out a fallow field nearby, which had been designated as a cemetery. Ordering my men to pitch camp on a meadow between two battle-scarred oaks, we made ourselves as comfortable as we could. The guns sounded much louder and we could see ambulances bringing the wounded to a field hospital.

Lieutenant Rutherford had urged me to have my men start work as soon as possible. By that evening, I had paced out the perimeter of the cemetery and we marked a neat grid. First thing next morning, we started excavating the graves. My men knew what was coming and so did I, but we busied ourselves as best we could, acting as if we were doing nothing more than digging more potholes to fill. Each pit was four feet deep and two and a half feet wide. Most of my men were farmers and they were used to working in the soil. By noon we had fifty graves ready when the first bodies began to arrive.

Though I cannot say for sure, it could have been the Irish regiment we'd seen three days before. None of the dead were recognizable. In most cases, the corpses had been torn to shreds by artillery shells and the wagons disgorged a gruesome assortment of limbs and torsos. Occasionally, something that looked like a man was unloaded and we lowered him into the ground on his own. Otherwise, we did the best we could, apportioning the remains. Soon enough, the first fifty graves had been filled. We sprinkled lime into each of the pits and shovelled earth on top of the dead, even as more bodies piled up. My men worked from dawn to dusk and they had no appetite in the evenings, though I forced them to eat and drink to keep up their strength. It was loathsome work but none of them complained. I could see the pain in their eyes, yet not a single expression of dissent. Whatever they had heard of European civilization must have seemed a terrible lie.

Over the next ten days, we buried more than 2,000 bodies, though it was impossible to keep count. By the end, the stench of decomposition had obliterated the odours of cordite, chlorine and mustard gas that blew in from the front. I never saw the officer who had asked about tigers and elephants again, but I assume he was one of the dead. Often, there was nothing left of a man except for a single boot with an anonymous foot inside, the rest of him blown to bits.

Even today I have nightmares and I'm sure every one of those men who came home with me suffered traumatic memories long after the Great War ended. While hunting man-eaters I have seen the mutilated remains of victims killed by tigers and leopards but nothing can compare to the savagery and desecration we witnessed on that field in France. Our labour corps was spared the enemy's bullets only to look death squarely in its hideous face, when mud and flesh become one substance and bones are shattered like sticks. I do not know if the commanding officer who gave us our orders survived the war or not. But if he did, and if he ever reads this account, I want him to know that my men were not mere '*coolies*'. They were unsung heroes who conducted themselves with resolute honour, showing utmost respect for the dead.

☘

Last year, Her Majesty Queen Elizabeth visited Kenya. She was still a princess then, and I was invited to accompany her and Prince Philip when they came to Treetops to photograph wildlife. After several hours observing elephants and other creatures on a salt lick they spent that night in the lodge, which is probably the most luxurious tree house ever built. By a tragic coincidence, King George VI, who was hunting grouse in Scotland, suddenly died in his sleep that same night. This sad news only reached the royal party after they had departed Treetops, but in the lodge register I recorded an account of their visit and concluded with a brief note:

> For the first time in the history of the world a young girl climbed into a tree one day a Princess, and after having what she described as her most thrilling experience she climbed down from the tree the next day a Queen—God bless her.

Despite the sorrowful ending, we enjoyed a magnificent time at Treetops and Her Highness took many photographs of rhinos, baboons and waterbuck. At one point in the afternoon, the princess turned to me and asked if I'd ever considered staying on in India after independence. I replied that having lived my entire life as a loyal subject of the British Crown, I had no intention of changing allegiances so late in life.

She laughed with a youthful brightness in her eyes. 'You're being diplomatic, Colonel Corbett,' she said. 'But I don't believe you for a moment. There must have been some other reason. Perhaps there were no tigers left for you to shoot.'

'Unfortunately, I'm no match for a tiger anymore, Your Highness,' I said. 'Though far fewer of them remain than in the days when I was hunting man-eaters.'

'I've read all of your books,' the princess said. 'Do you know which one I like the best?'

Flattered, I could only bow my head and smile.

'*My India*,' she said, which surprised me, for I thought the princess would choose one of the tiger books instead, 'because it tells the stories of ordinary people and you obviously know so much about them and feel compassion for the poor.'

'It's very kind of you to say that, Your Highness,' I replied.

'The title caught my interest right away,' she said. 'It is *your* India, of course, but you don't lay any claim to it. I thought it was a very honest book but it made me wonder why you would choose to leave, when you obviously love that country as much as you do.'

'With independence everything was changing,' I said. 'It was no longer *my* India and, I suppose, I didn't have the courage to see it change.'

'But countries don't really change, do they?' she said, with a quizzical look. 'It's only the people at the top.'

I was about to respond when two wildebeest came trotting up to the salt lick, shaking their ungainly heads. Immediately, the princess picked up her camera and began to photograph them from her perch in the tree. And I was greatly relieved that I wouldn't be forced to answer a question for which I had no ready reply.

A little while later, Prince Philip and I retreated to another balcony, where I had a cigarette, for I still hold onto this pernicious habit or rather it holds onto to me. As we were chatting about wildlife, the Duke of Edinburgh asked me what I made of the 'so-called sixth sense', and whether it could be a primal instinct inherited from our ancient ancestors who hunted and gathered on these wild and fertile plains.

In response to Prince Philip's question, I recounted a story that illustrates the importance of heeding our sixth sense. The tale relates an encounter I had with a Himalayan brown bear. This animal is virtually identical to the red bears of Europe and Russia and closely related to the grizzly that strikes terror in the hearts of trappers and homesteaders in the wilder parts of North America.

Both the brown bear, *Ursus arctos,* and its smaller black brother, *Selenarctos thibetanus*, are unpredictable and dangerous animals, largely on account of poor eyesight. Once, when I was hunting near the Pindari Glacier, I had gone for an early morning walk along a high altitude meadow near a forest rest house called Dhakuri. It was a bright, clear morning and the snow peaks were visible to the north. My heart was racing not only from the altitude but from the sheer exhilaration of being alive in that highland paradise. As the sun came up, a feeling of awe and well-being washed over me. I could hear monal pheasants calling along the wooded margins of the meadows, which were embroidered with wildflowers.

Yet suddenly a shadow seemed to fall across my path and my exuberance was choked by a feeling of dread and alarm. On the surface nothing had changed in the landscape to make me aware of danger but, all at once, I felt an overwhelming premonition telling me to turn around or take another path. After several minutes of hesitation, debating what to do, I chose to ignore my fears and kept going. A hundred yards on, I turned a corner of the ridge and came upon a large brown bear feasting on a bush covered with yellow raspberries. Though bears cannot see clearly, they have a keen sense of smell and good hearing. Either my footsteps or my scent must have alarmed him and he screamed with rage.

The only weapon I was carrying was a 12-bore shotgun. My

object that day was bagging a monal or koklas pheasant for dinner. Both barrels were loaded with No. 6 birdshot, which would have done no more damage to the bear than a swarm of stinging gnats. The sound of the gun going off might have scared him but he was so furious at my intrusion that I had little confidence it would deter him and might even hasten his advance. Several tall trees stood nearby that I could have climbed. In those days I was young enough to scramble from limb to limb with the alacrity of my primate ancestors. Yet I knew the bear was far better at this than I and he would have easily torn my legs to shreds before I shinnied halfway up the trunk.

Understanding that his eyesight was weak, I realized the bear had formed an opinion of me based on other senses. What he probably saw in front of him was a fuzzy bipedal figure that vaguely resembled a man. For him, I represented a natural enemy, whether he could see me or not. Others must have fired muzzle-loaders at this bear and he hadn't forgotten old injuries or the distinctive odour of his would-be assassins. With this half-formed impression in his mind the bear flung himself off the raspberry bush and stood up on his hind legs, as if he were imitating my stance. I saw his claws, his teeth and small, dull eyes. In another thirty seconds, he would have torn me apart, as bears often do with human trespassers, embracing their victims and then ripping them open with their claws. The truth is most Himalayan residents fear bears more than leopards or tigers, for *Ursus* is not a calculating killer but a short-tempered, unpredictable brute like us.

In that brief interval, while I still had a choice of how to respond, I made a quick decision to lower my gun to the ground and cup both hands around my mouth. Taking the deepest breath I could inhale, I roared like a tiger. As many of my readers may know, I have demonstrated this call on numerous occasions, usually in a classroom full of schoolchildren. The roar of a tiger has a chilling effect on every creature, large or small, for there is no other sound like it in the forest. At close quarters a tiger's roar resonates with our deepest fears. I had practised it for many years, until I was able to

successfully call tigers in the wild, bringing them within ten yards
of my hide. Therefore, that morning in the Upper Himalayas, when
I made the chance acquaintance of this shaggy brown-haired beast,
the call I emitted was the loudest and most convincing rendition
of a male tiger that I could muster.

Brown bears and tigers live at different altitudes and he had
probably never heard such a sound before but clearly understood
that this was something more than he had bargained for. His reaction
would have been comical, had it not been a matter of life and
death. I could have sworn he blinked his eyes a couple of times,
as if trying to focus and wishing he had worn his spectacles. The
ferocious demeanour suddenly wilted and he let out a whimpering
grunt. Dropping to all fours, the bear immediately turned tail and
bolted off down the ridge like a dog being chased by an angry cloud
of bees. For good measure I let loose another roar but by then the
bear was long gone, heading for his cave in the valley, no doubt.

When I picked up my shotgun, I found both of my hands
were trembling so badly I couldn't have hit a bear broadside if I
tried. Sitting down on a boulder nearby to ease the knocking of
my knees, I calmed my nerves as I made a quick breakfast of the
yellow raspberries that the bear had kindly left behind.

Because of this experience and countless others I certainly believe
that our 'sixth sense' is an early warning system braided into our
genes. It may well have been part of the psychology of primitive
hunters but it is as relevant today as it was so many thousands of
years ago, when our survival depended upon it.

Perhaps it is a hunter's instincts that have brought me here to
Kenya, all the way from the foothills of the Himalayas where I was
born, to these alien escarpments in Africa where I will probably die.
Though I seldom carry a gun any more, and buy my guinea fowl
and meat from a butcher shop rather than stalking wild game, those
primal instincts remain. We hunt in order to perpetuate our species,
even as we face the inevitability of extinction. In this process the
truest and most admirable traits we possess are inherited from our
animal nature. It isn't reason or religion that makes us a successful

species, or the literature we read in school, or the patriotic discipline and dedication with which we defend our nation's interests. Instead, it is the primitive impulses we follow, which have been with us from our earliest incarnations. Whatever we may have become, *Homo sapiens* were once nothing more than lonely hunters with no sense of right or wrong but only a feeling inside our marrow that somehow we must carry on. In that simple equation lies our sole claim to nobility and virtue. The survival of our species is the only moral choice we face.

At the same time, we share an affinity with wild creatures both in reality and in our imaginations. The stories we tell often attribute human characteristics to animals, as Mr Kipling has done in his fanciful but amusing *Jungle Book*. But we are equally fascinated by that mysterious, unnamed creature that skulks beneath our skin. Fables of Romulus and Remus, or the ancient Sumerian epic of Gilgamesh, in which a half-man half-beast called Enkidu roams the steppes, all point towards our feral instincts. In fact, we need look no farther than the New Testament in which John the Baptist retreats from human society, donning animal skins and feeding on wild fruits and honey. St John in the Wilderness is an ascetic prophet who announces the imminent arrival of a messiah but also calls us back to our primitive roots from which we have wandered astray.

꙰

Fear has always been my constant companion throughout a life spent in the jungle, though I have learned to control it as best I can. The terror that stalks us at night is often nothing more than a figment of our imagination. When I was younger I was less afraid, for youth thrives on a naive sense of invincibility, and in those days I had fewer experiences to make me cautious. Now, as my mortality becomes more evident with each passing hour, I have come to accept that fear is a normal part of human nature and must not be denied. It protects us in many ways, warning of the dangers that surround us but also alerting us to those insidious threats within, the haunting memories that keep returning with unwarranted persistence.

As a hunter and a naturalist, I have spent most of my life in the wild and many of my encounters with large predators should have made me wary of every sound and shadow—the snapping of a twig, the rustle of a leaf. But there is no place where I have felt safer and more secure than in the jungles of India, because I understood the language of wild creatures and learned to read the signs around me. When I speak in public about these experiences, often to groups of schoolchildren, I try to explain how I received my education in jungle lore and did my homework, diligently memorizing each lesson. The alarm calls of babblers and barking deer announcing a tiger's presence reassure me rather than being a source of terror, because they tell us exactly where danger lies. When I see fresh pugmarks crossing my path it reveals which animal it is and where it is going. The cries I hear in the forest are as reliable as sworn testimony in a magistrate's court—a langur calling out to tell others that he has seen a leopard pass beneath his perch or the noisy chatter of laughingthrushes signalling 'all clear'. In my experience, birds and beasts seldom lie and I have grown to trust their voices more than human conversation.

Two experiences, in particular, at different points in my life, reveal to me the constancy of nature as well as the unreliability of our own species. The first occurred when I was still a boy. The murder of a young woman in Nainital had been blamed on a leopard. Eventually, the truth came out, ten years after her death, when the victim's grave was desecrated. The leopard in question had been killed long ago, though it was clearly not a man-eater. By accident, I happened to witness the second act of this crime. At a young, impressionable age I learned how collective opinion, especially in a small town like Nainital, can be swayed by emotion and prejudice rather than deliberate investigation or a clear appreciation of facts.

The second incident took place more than thirty years later, when I was asked to hunt down a man-eater near a place called Mayaghat along the Sarda River, which forms the border between India and Nepal. It was, at the time, a remote and unsettled part of Kumaon, full of tigers and plenty of prey. The only people who lived here were forest dwellers known as Banrajis, or 'kings of the jungle'. They were hunters and gatherers like our earliest ancestors and lived in harmony with nature, free of the trappings of civilization. In 1926, the forests of this region were marked for felling to produce timber for the Indian Railways.

Teams of labourers, brought up from the plains to clear the forest, were attacked by a tiger that killed six victims before I arrived. Though it was obviously a man-eater, superstition and prejudice intervened and many believed it was a demon taking revenge for the destruction of the jungle. I was told that I would never be able to exterminate this tiger because it was protected by supernatural powers. In the end, of course, the man-eater turned out to be an old tigress with an injured leg and broken teeth. I shot her over the remains of her last victim and put an end to her depredations but it was the Banrajis who paid the ultimate price. Forest department officials, who saw them as poachers and 'vermin', were determined to drive them out of the jungle, which had been their home for generations. The violence that occurred and the loss of innocent lives made me understand how men in power have little regard for those who are poor and helpless. The horrors of war demonstrate the brutality of human conflict, yet even in peace time the ruthless actions of men who claim to be following orders lead to horrific atrocities, disguised in the name of progress.

᪲

For the most part, I have abandoned my guns in favour of the camera, which affords me far greater pleasure and a more satisfying sense of accomplishment in the jungle. This transition began many years ago when I realized the exciting challenges of wildlife photography. Around that time, F. W. Champion had published his books, *With a Camera in Tiger-land* and *The Jungle in Sunlight and Shadow*. By then my youthful excitement over killing animals had worn off and I preferred to enter the jungle as a silent observer, trying to make myself as invisible as possible so that I could approach animals at close quarters. I had also realized that marksmanship is a finite art that can only be perfected up to a point, after which hitting the bullseye becomes a futile exercise of putting one hole inside another.

Rifles are crude mechanisms designed to detonate an explosive charge that sends a lump of lead hurtling through the air. Leaf sights can be adjusted to compensate for distance but beyond that there is little subtlety or nuance, whereas a camera requires careful measurement of light, the calibration of f-stops and shutter speeds down to a hundredth of a second, gauging focus and depth of field, as well as the overall frame of the picture. A well-placed bullet goes straight to the heart or brain, while a photograph takes in the whole creature as well as its surroundings. Being armed with a camera makes us tread more lightly and select our targets with greater precision. And, in the end, what we capture on film will last far longer than moth-eaten trophies.

For a naturalist, one of the greatest attractions of wildlife photography is that it gives us an opportunity to test our intuition in the forest to a degree that hunting seldom does. I have learned far greater levels of patience while trying to film tigers in the wild than I ever did when stalking man-eaters. Yet the same instincts and skills are employed. I listen for the sounds of the predator's approach, the nattering of birds that suddenly turn to screams of warning, crushed blades of grass springing up seconds after an animal has stepped on them, drops of blood on a leaf and drag marks in the sand. All these signals alert me to a tiger's presence so that I can position myself and be prepared for that moment when the object of my quest appears within the viewfinder.

Mr Champion achieved wonderful results with flash photography, setting up his cameras with automatic triggers, so that the wariest of creatures took their own portraits. I have had less luck with this and the best photographs I have taken were the result of calling animals into view. The moaning roar of a tigress in search of a willing consort is something I learned to imitate years ago. It is the most effective means of tempting eligible bachelors into range. Soon after I bought my first camera, I hid myself behind a ber or jujube bush (*Ziziphus jujuba*) overlooking a dry watercourse in the jungle near our home in Kaladhungi. Several male tigers lived in the vicinity and I was determined to lure one of them with the mating call of a tigress in heat.

By the third call, I received an amorous reply. The male tiger was approximately half a mile away but approaching rapidly down the dry watercourse that led to my thorny hide. Making final adjustments to my camera, I readied myself for the shot and let out another seductive moan. Immediately, I received an answer but this time from the opposite side, about a quarter mile to my right, where I knew there was a dense growth of bamboo. Before I could repeat my call, this roar was echoed by the tiger to my left and I realized I had summoned two male tigers at once, each of whom must have imagined a beautiful mistress awaiting him in her leafy bower. Against my better judgement, but thinking only of the dramatic photograph I might be able to take, I let out another bellowing 'come hither'. Foolishly, I had left my rifle at home and was armed only with a small pocketknife, its blade about the length of a tiger's claw. By now the two males had heard each other and from the tone of their roars I could tell they were preparing to fight a duel to the death, in which I was the prize. As they came closer, I began to wish I had chosen a tree to sit up in, rather than being stranded on the ground, but it was too late to shift my position.

The first tiger soon made an appearance. He was a young, full-grown male who strode into the middle of the watercourse about twenty feet away and emptied his lungs with a passionate declaration of desire. Instantly, from the opposite side, and a bit farther away, an even larger tiger entered the arena. I recognized him as the dominant male in our forest, for I had seen his giant pugmarks often and he had crossed my path several times during the winter months. Earlier estimates placed his size at ten feet, measured over the curves, but seeing him now at close quarters, I added another six inches at least. He was enormous and from his stance I could see that he was expecting to find his Beatrice or Josephine close at hand. Fortunately for me the two male tigers distracted each other, at least for a moment, tensing and flexing their muscles, preparing for combat.

Not wanting to be the cause of courtship violence, I stood up very slowly and pointed my camera at the larger male, who spotted me before the shutter clicked. Through the lens I could see anger and disappointment in his eyes. He had been expecting a svelte young lady in furs but instead here was an underfed, rather mangy-looking Englishman. Sudden movements often prompt a charge, so I turned very slowly to see what his opponent thought of the situation. Once again, through the viewfinder, I focused on a confused and startled tiger who had been prepared to fight for love and honour. Now that the stakes had been lowered he wasn't so sure. If this had been an opera it was my turn for an aria but I had lost all enthusiasm for mating calls and if I had tried to roar it would have come out as an apologetic whimper.

Fortunately, the situation was saved by a peacock, which had been watching our charade from a semal tree nearby and was probably wondering what sort of madman would call up two tigers at once. The suspense must have been unbearable for the peacock who let out a loud 'miaow' and flew off in a bluster of wings. Ordinarily a tiger wouldn't have been bothered by a peafowl but the sudden sound sent both of my suitors slinking away in opposite directions, leaving me alone at the altar.

As a postscript, a week later, when I had the photographs developed the results were disappointing. My hands had been shaking so hard both images of the tigers were blurred.

⁕

The reliability of photography has improved considerably since I acquired my first camera. Telephoto lenses and faster speed films have made it possible to achieve remarkable results. Kodak has refined its colour processing so that we can now replicate nature in all its variegated hues, not simply in shades of black and white. This has aided an amateur like me and I have become a willing and eager convert to new technologies, especially in cinematography where lighter and simpler cameras make it possible to take moving pictures in the wild. But even with a 16mm Bell & Howell Filmo 75, nature holds its mysteries close to her chest and I have found, on rare occasions, that a camera has failed me. For all its miraculous advances, we must accept that photography has its limits. Efforts at taking a snapshot of the Loch Ness monster or the yeti have yielded indifferent results. Even with well-known species there is sometimes a significant gap between reality and perception. As an example, I will relate one final incident that occurred on 6 June 1945, when I attempted to film a leopard with a cine camera, a few miles above Kaladhungi on the walking road up to Nainital.

Leopards are more difficult to photograph than tigers because they are almost entirely nocturnal. Even when they come out at dawn or dusk there is seldom enough light for satisfactory results. But I had received reports about a certain leopard who was particularly bold and made a habit of crossing the Kaladhungi-Nainital Road at all hours of the day. He had killed several cows and goats in a village called Teetarpatti and for the past two months the farmers there had been pleading with me to shoot him, saying they feared he might become a man-eater. Thrice he had aggressively confronted human beings, though none of his attacks was fatal. Until then I had refused to kill him but I felt it would be unfair to the villagers if I went armed only with my camera, so I decided to sit up for the leopard, attempting to film him first but with the secondary objective of ridding the village of this cattle-lifter who would, soon enough, acquire a taste for human flesh.

Purchasing one of the surviving goats, I tied a bell around its throat and tethered it to a tree on a densely forested stretch of the road, about a mile above the village. Being summer, there was a fair amount of coming and going, with trains of mules and porters carrying produce and provisions up the hill to Nainital. Most of this activity stopped by 4 p.m., which is when I took up my position in the ruins of an old dharamshala, which hadn't been used for twenty years. It was originally built by a wealthy trader from Ramnagar at the insistence of a rishi who acted as the caretaker and ministered to pilgrims en route to Badrinath. The rishi later died on the spot when an earthquake toppled the walls and slate roof, after which the place acquired an inauspicious reputation. Jungle lay all around and a tangle of bauhinia vines covered most of the ruins, providing me with a sheltered spot where I set up my tripod and camera to film the leopard if he chose to pounce on my goat.

Next to the dharamshala was a spring that suited my purposes. Though it was only a trickle at this time of year, I was able to direct the flow through a bamboo spout so it splashed against the rocks, creating enough noise to drown out the whirring of my cine-camera when I switched it on. Everything was in position and the goat cooperated by bleating and tugging at its tether so the bell around its neck rang out in the stillness of the forest. I felt sure that if the leopard was anywhere within earshot, he would certainly pay us a visit. The rifle I was carrying was a light .275 Rigby-Mauser, presented to me in 1907 by Sir J. P. Hewitt, then Governor of the United Provinces, in appreciation for my shooting the Champawat man-eater. It was more than adequate for a leopard though I was primarily interested in getting footage of him attacking the goat rather than putting an end to his reign.

A leopard's call is very different from a tiger's. Sometimes described as 'sawing', it has a rasping resonance, as if a log were being cut in half. As I have grown older and my vocal chords less supple, I find it more difficult to produce a convincing rendition. For this reason, I remained silent that day and let the goat's pathetic cries and the tinkling bell make its presence known. An hour passed and nothing happened until gradually the light began to fade. I listened attentively to the 'jungle telegraph', a communications system that enlists a multitude of species from red junglefowl that crowed in the valley to the sneezing of goral on the cliffs above. From all reports, the news was peaceful—a steady metallic tempo of coppersmith barbets and the contented burbling of doves. But then, off in the distance, I heard the panicked screech of a kalij pheasant heralding the movement of a predator. Soon enough, others picked it up and passed on the word until a flock of jungle babblers began spreading noisy gossip that a leopard was on the prowl.

I had set up my cine-camera in such a way that it focused on a corner of the road approaching the dharamshala from the northeast. Removing the lens cap to avoid any unnecessary movement later on, I put my finger on the trigger. The babblers had seven more sisters closer by and these too set up a raucous alarm. Seconds later, I saw a shape emerge from the underbrush and the leopard stepped out onto the road and came towards me at a slow, deliberate pace. The light was limited but, as the camera began to purr, I could make out the dark pattern of rosettes and the tawny amber of his fur. He was an old leopard, well past his prime, with a limp in his left foreleg. I expected him to crouch and then spring on the goat but instead he stopped and sat down for a moment as if posing for my camera of which he seemed entirely unaware. I only wished the sun had been shining on him for there were shadows from the trees and his camouflaged coat blended in with the patterns of dark and light. He made no sound, studying the bait for sixty seconds or more then rising again. But instead of advancing on the goat, which had fallen silent in terror, he abruptly turned aside and disappeared into the trees. I waited several minutes, letting the camera run and hoping he would attack from cover, but nothing happened beyond the cry of a startled black partridge fifty yards to my right.

At this point I realized the leopard had no interest in killing the goat. Perhaps he had eaten recently or his appetite had turned to wilder fare. Remembering my promise to the villagers, I switched off the camera and picked up my rifle. Giving the goat a reassuring scratch between its horns, I went to the spot where the leopard had vanished and saw a game track entering the jungle. For a hundred yards or more, the route was mostly level and then the trail, such as it was, climbed up the steep flank of the ridge. I kept an eye out for pugmarks but there was too much leaf litter on the ground. All around me lay dense foliage and I began to realize the foolish risk I was taking. If this leopard was, in fact, aggressive then he held a considerable advantage over me. Adding to this, all my correspondents in the jungle had fallen silent—not a bird call or the cry of a deer to help me out. Even the goat, which had been frantically bleating and ringing its bell after my departure, was no longer making a sound.

After three quarters of an hour, in which I covered four hundred yards at most, I decided to turn around. Retracing my steps along the game track, I made by way back to the dharamshala. To my utter surprise, I saw that the goat was gone. Releasing the safety catch on my rifle I moved carefully forward, seeing the tether still attached to the tree. The leopard must have circled back and carried off the goat, but when I examined the rope it wasn't broken or frayed and there was no blood on the ground or any sign of a struggle. All I could figure was that the knot I'd tied had come loose and the goat had slipped free, though I remained puzzled as I collected my camera and set off for the village. Sure enough, when I got there, the goat was waiting for me, having happily found its way home.

By the time I reached Kaladhungi the stars were out and the temperature had dropped a degree or two. It was summer and miserably hot so I hardly slept at all beneath a mosquito net. Still baffled by the experience I kept wondering why the leopard had turned down a free meal. The next morning, setting off for Nainital, I passed the spot again and stopped to see if I could read anything in the dust but by then several mule trains had passed along the road and I could find no tracks, except my own.

In those days I used to send my cine-film to a laboratory in Bombay for developing and it took about a month to process. When the film came back I immediately opened the package and set up my 16mm projector in the drawing room of Gurney House. One of Maggie's old tablecloths was tacked to the wall as a screen. Threading the film through the sprocket I switched on the lamp and let it run. To begin with there were a few earlier shots I'd taken of a young elephant who had broken into our orchard in Kaladhungi. Then the sequence with the leopard began, except I found that he wasn't there. I could see the road and the surrounding trees, with shadows swaying in the breeze. The goat stood in the foreground, securely tied to the tree but that was all. No leopard made an appearance though I watched the film several times.

I know for certain what I saw that day and in my mind I can

still clearly picture the leopard stepping into view and approaching along the road, then sitting down to study the goat before vanishing into the jungle. Yet the film revealed none of this, not even a hint of the leopard, as if I'd imagined it all.

My memory may be called into question, but I am willing to swear on whatever holy books are at hand that a leopard walked down that road and stood thirty feet from me, as I watched it through the viewfinder of my camera. Should anyone suggest another explanation I can assure them that I had consumed nothing stronger than a cup of tea in the village and I was not suffering from delusional fevers. I know what I saw. But to this day I cannot explain what occurred and why the camera failed to record the leopard's presence. Sometimes, I still wake up at night and wonder who untied that goat...

Looking out my window, I can see that it is getting late and the sun is setting beyond the acacia trees at the edge of our yard in Nyeri. Many more stories remain to be told about tracking animals with a camera. A few of the pictures I have taken might even be worth a thousand words, but I have already tested the patience of my readers and I can hear Maggie saying, 'Go on, Jim, get to the point!' Like any campfire raconteur, I've rambled and digressed. But now, I suppose, I must sum it all up with some sort of opinion or pronouncement like those well-informed gentlemen who write letters to *The Times*.

On the wall above my desk is a black and white photograph from 1926 taken in the Sarda Valley of eastern Kumaon, where I had gone to hunt the Mayaghat man-eater. It is a simple scene of a riverbank with forest all around and a small stream entering the larger river. A woman carrying a water vessel on her head is coming towards me. She is frozen in time by the camera's shutter. The landscape is almost abstract in its simplicity, yet I find this picture still evokes an incurable ache of longing in me for the wild beauty of those Indian jungles where I spent so much of my life.

This photograph is more than a memory, closer to a dream. It is one of the few things I brought with me to Kenya. So much was left behind—books, trophies, furniture—all of it sold off in the muddled haste of departure. But, somehow, this image has travelled with me and speaks of origins, the verdant sanctuary out of which I've come. When I look at the riffled current of the river, swelling over a submerged boulder and recognize a tall silk-cotton tree raising its head above the swathe of foliage that lies across the river, suddenly I am a boy again, ten or twelve years old, setting off into the forest alone. I can hear a brainfever bird calling and in the sand are fresh prints of deer and tiger, boar and leopard. It is a peaceable kingdom, yet full of danger and excitement for a boy that age, who holds an old muzzle-loader in both hands imagining himself to be Hawk Eye, the fearless tracker, setting off in search of unknown frontiers.

When I think of that boy he seems no different from me at this age, now seventy-eight, though I could no longer keep up with him and my eyesight is failing, so that the jungle becomes a green blur. Only one of my ears can be trusted these days and even my sense of smell has been dulled with age. The only faculty that hasn't diminished with time is my sixth sense. Somehow, I can still conjure up that acute combination of fear and excitement I often experienced when setting foot in an unfamiliar forest, reading the telltale signs around me, knowing that a predator was nearby.

The indistinct figure of the woman, too far away in the picture for me to see her face, sways gracefully as she walks towards the camera. *Who is she?* I ask myself. What would that boy have said to her if they had met? *Is she a goddess?* Kaiyu Devi, a woodland deity worshipped by tribal hunters, the maternal spirit of the jungle? At his age, the boy doesn't care about these things, though he feels a shared loneliness in her presence. She lives by herself in a hut near the river and leads him home, laughing at his shy manner. They speak the same language and instinctively the boy feels as if he's known her all his life. He tells her things about himself that nobody else would understand, secrets confessed in a forest tongue, whispers amongst the leaves.

All this I see in the photograph, which brings me back to Her

Majesty's persistent question: *Why did I leave?* Why couldn't I have simply stayed on in India and lived out the last few years of my life within the familiar embrace of those jungles where I grew up and discovered what mattered most? Of course, it is too late to regret my decision. Going back to India now would be much worse than leaving in the first place.

My India has disappeared forever and I cannot reclaim it. We must live with the choices we make. But perhaps it wasn't a choice at all but rather my sixth sense that told me it was time to go, a raw nerve that raised an alarm, a quickening pulse like an extra heartbeat between two seconds on the clock, that primal instinct for survival passed down through our ancestral genes when a hunter finally knows the game is up.

IV
IN MEMORIAM

Jim Corbett died of a heart attack at the age of seventy-nine in 1955. He was buried in the cemetery of St Peter's Church in Nyeri, Kenya. His sister, Maggie, survived him by eight years and died in 1963. Her ashes were interred in the same grave as her brother. Their stone bears the following inscription:

IN FOND REMEMBRANCE
OF
EDWARD JAMES (JIM) CORBETT
BORN IN NAINI TAL, INDIA
25TH JULY, 1875
DIED IN NYERI
19TH APRIL, 1955

UNTIL THE DAY BREAK, AND
THE SHADOWS FLEE AWAY

HIS SISTER MAGGIE
26-12-1963

The brief line of verse engraved on this tomb is identical to the inscription on their mother's gravestone in the St John in the Wilderness cemetery, Nainital. It comes from the second Song of Solomon in the King James Version of the Bible:

I am the rose of Sharon, and the lily of the valleys.
As the lily among thorns, so is my love among the daughters.
As the apple tree among the trees of the wood, so is my beloved among the sons. I sat down under his shadow with great delight, and his fruit was sweet to my taste.
He brought me to the banqueting house, and his banner over

me was love.

Stay me with flagons, comfort me with apples: for I am sick of love.

His left hand is under my head, and his right hand doth embrace me.

I charge you, O ye daughters of Jerusalem, by the roes, and by the hinds of the field, that ye stir not up, nor awake my love, till he please.

The voice of my beloved! behold, he cometh leaping upon the mountains, skipping upon the hills.

My beloved is like a roe or a young hart: behold, he standeth behind our wall, he looketh forth at the windows, shewing himself through the lattice.

My beloved spake, and said unto me, Rise up, my love, my fair one, and come away.

For, lo, the winter is past, the rain is over and gone;

The flowers appear on the earth; the time of the singing of birds is come, and the voice of the turtle is heard in our land; The fig tree putteth forth her green figs, and the vines with the tender grape give a good smell. Arise, my love, my fair one, and come away.

O my dove, that art in the clefts of the rock, in the secret places of the stairs, let me see thy countenance, let me hear thy voice; for sweet is thy voice, and thy countenance is comely.

Take us the foxes, the little foxes, that spoil the vines: for our vines have tender grapes.

My beloved is mine, and I am his: he feedeth among the lilies. Until the day break, and the shadows flee away, turn, my beloved, and be thou like a roe or a young hart upon the mountains of Bether.

SOURCES

While this novel is a work of fiction, many of the characters and situations are based on historical and biographical facts. A few dates and locations have been adjusted. Among the sources I consulted, Jim Corbett's own writings and D. C. Kala's account of Corbett's life provided most of the inspiration and detail. Published works that I have drawn from are listed below:

Corbett, Jim, *Jungle Lore,* Bombay: OUP, 1953.

————*Jungle Stories,* Nainital (privately published by the author), 1935.

————*Man-eaters of Kumaon,* Bombay: OUP, 1944.

————*My India,* Bombay: OUP, 1952.

————*The Man-eating Leopard of Rudraprayag,* Bombay: OUP, 1947.

————*The Temple Tiger and More Man-eaters of Kumaon,* Bombay: OUP, 1955.

————*Tree Tops,* Bombay: OUP, 1955.

Fortier, Jana, *Kings of the Forest: The Cultural Resilience of Himalayan Hunter-Gatherers,* Honolulu: University of Hawai'i Press, 2009.

Hawkins, R. E., ed. *Jim Corbett's India*, Delhi: Oxford, 1978.

Kala, D. C., *Jim Corbett of Kumaon,* Delhi: Penguin & Ravi Dayal, 2009.